Moonlight in Lalibela

By JR Dickey

Index

Author's Note

This is a fictional story, but it is based upon a true, life experience of the author as well as the writings of Daniel, Ezekiel, John and other Biblical prophecy. The central character really did have the life-changing encounter with his Lord in a similar fashion as described herein. Nearly all names are of real people but have been modified. They do not imply any person's projected involvement in actual future or current events.

This is the first of three stories that culminate with what the Apostle Paul described as "life from the dead" and a glorious future. However, the path to that promise will undoubtedly test our faith.

The prophecies may not come to pass as the story portrays but they will come to pass. How soon? Some believe they have already begun.

JR Dickey

Cast of Characters

Abdul Mahgoub – 48 years old, legitimately elected Prime Minister of Sudan. Author, poet, statesman, Allamah in Islam

Aliya Mahgoub – 38 years old, wife of Abdul.

Amir – 42 years old, Lt. General and Commander of the Baghdad Operational Command

Ari Rosen – 59 years old, Prime Minister of Israel

Ashfin – 39 years old, Iranian General in charge of Quds, from southern Iran

Aziz – 60 years old, father in law to Abdul, principle Allamah in Islam

Amani Mahgoub – young son of Abdul

Baruch – 40 years old, high ranking General in Israel's IDF, Council member

Berenike – 37 years old, high ranking General in Egyptian Army, Council member

Faheema Mahgoub – young daughter of Abdul

Ibrahim – 42 years old, Saudi Prince, Council member

Ismail – Age unknown, Libyan/Iraqi, protégé of the Leader, Chief Administrator of the Council

James – 32 years old, American, friend to Abdul

Michael – 12 years old, James' son

Naryshkin – 48 years old, Director of Russian SVR and confidante to Russian President

Parolin – age unknown, Italian/Jew, Vatican Secretary of State

Sisi – 60 years old, President of Egypt, jealous adversary of Abdul

Tamar Mintz – 30 years old, Israeli, Chief Data Scientist in IDF's Cyber Defense Directorate

Talia Dahan – 36 years old, Major, Pilot in IAF

Tasha – 3 years old, daughter of James and Vanessa, real name Starshine

The Leader – age unknown, origin thought to be town near ancient Babylon, founder of Council

Vanessa – 32 years old, Israeli Jewish Christian, wife of James and mother of Tasha

Yaakov Katz – 40 years old, Lt. Col. in Israel's IAF, Commander and Pilot

Yehuda – 38 years old, Mossad unit Director and experienced assassin, Council member

Prologue

It all started with a dream. At first, it terrified, then gradually like a small seed planted in the mind of a child, its dark alluring influence grew to shape the boy's mind – his goals, his destiny and his devotion to establishing unparalleled greatness in the world. As he grew, every door to persuasion, wealth and power opened to him effortlessly. Emerging from the depths of obscurity, he relentlessly focused on developing a secretive ever-expanding network of like-minded 'elite.'

He never really knew his father, but rumor had it that he was violently insane, and his mother was as vile a person as ever existed. The only thing they instilled in him was the inclination to hate, and the only thing he ultimately cared about was to lead. At the age of 30, he came to understand why.

Chapter 1

Khartoum, Kobers military jail cell. 2:30 AM

It was dark, dank and freakishly cold. Echoing in the hallway, tortured screams alternating between whimpering and emphatic pleas for mercy added to the heavy sense of hopelessness of this place. Abdul expected to be next. His cell and the cells around him had been filled with 'insurrectionists' and 'traitors'. Now, they were empty except for Mohamed who was on the floor next to him, and the stench of death was overwhelming.

His body ached terribly from the earlier beatings and he couldn't prevent his mind from riveting its focus on the bloody dismembered bodies of his friends that he saw as he was dragged to this hole.

Everything had happened so fast. He was not prepared to die; the thought terrified him. The security forces he relied upon had vanished or turned on him with a startling vengeance. Now, with no food or water or 'facilities' for what seemed like several days, his mind was spinning with fears, suspicions and questions. Who? Why? How?

He knew Khartoum jails were not designed with rehabilitation in mind. However, whoever was in control of his country now was using them to eliminate all opposition.

Suddenly, a series of thunderous explosions shook the building. The ensuing clamor of the guards diverted his attention from his scratching on the wall. He knew what he was doing was pointless, but for some reason it gave him a purpose in this morbid cell and assuaged his nihilism. He was almost finished with it - a very brief but symbolic will.

Aliya was the one who always kept him focused on things that mattered. Abdul loved her more and more deeply even as his life took on heavier and more consuming responsibilities. He could always count on her to be logical and practical which he figured was a good balance to his 'head in the clouds' ambitions and hopes. In fact, that was one of the reasons they had named their first boy Amani and their first girl Faheema.

As with all Sudanese, his family was very dear to Abdul, but they were also the ones who truly motivated him, who inspired him to serve Allah so passionately.

They had known each other as children though she was younger. As a wild young man, Abdul saw her as a little girl who tagged along when she could. He had no idea how much she adored him. As she became a woman, he was about to be off to engineering school, but her beauty struck him and stuck with him. He had no parents to visit but when he returned to see after his brother, he made excuses to also see Aliya and each time, her eyes, her smile, her charm enchanted him further. She was the most beautiful, perfect woman God created, or so he thought.

She had her own mind and was fiercely courageous in a culture that brutally kept her gender in its place. But her heart had always been his. Her father, on the other hand, did not think much of the idea of this rebellious young man becoming his son. She pleaded with him for openness to Abdul, the love of her life, but he stubbornly refused to consider it until Abdul finally returned from his schooling. That's when things suddenly changed, and she didn't care why. Aziz began to welcome Abdul, to encourage him to write and eventually to speak publicly.

Here in the cell, his mind raced. Were they safe? Did they know where he was and that no matter what happened, that he loved them? He longed to hear Aliya's encouragement one more time and to hold Amani and Faheema. Aziz was another matter. His father-in-law was a principle Allamah as was Abdul. Both had accomplished much in the name of Islam.

Aziz's influence, however, over Aliya was still considerable, such that even as Abdul had acquired greater and greater notoriety and political power, he had instructed her to keep a close eye on his son-in-law's devotion. Abdul admired Aziz, but always knew his harsh and distrusting eyes were constantly upon him.

Even now, though his head ached terribly, and his thinking was clouded by the pain, he suspected the insurrection and overthrow of his new government was driven by the Brotherhood to which Aziz had very close ties.

Aziz was a rock. His face chiseled from sandstone covered by a wiry graying beard and his heart from black marble. He knew the Quran better than Abdul and always held that over him. For years he had been an immoveable obstacle for the young man and then suddenly became his mentor and guide. Aziz knew everyone, everyone who mattered. Abdul welcomed the change in attitude but never truly trusted him. It was Aziz who had the connections and who began for some mysterious reason urging him to "do all the right things." How did he have the money to get Abdul into the right circles? How did he know what these "right things" were? Abdul never knew. Aziz remained an enigma.

Startlingly, as these thoughts swirled around, he began to wonder if his passion for serving Allah was as much his own as it may have been nurtured, even driven, by those ever present 'eyes'. They haunted him.

Abdul was a poet and a writer; his poetry exalted Allah while his writing critically examined democracy in the Arab world. Of course, He believed, but he also had questions. Over the last decade or so, he had published, proclaimed and presided; he had enjoyed what he considered divine purpose and an important standing in Islam and in the Arab world. Yet he thirsted inwardly for something he could not define. 'Only Allah can define it', he surmised. For as long as he could remember, it was a 'nagging' thought he never discussed. Nevertheless, his writing, his drive for political power and reform was all tied somehow to his desire for answers to the undefined.

Orphaned very early, Abdul had few memories of his childhood but was insatiable in his personal quest to make a difference, to have a relevant life. He remembered the malaria like seeing through a fog. He remembered stumbling out of his bed feverish and starving and seeing both his parents, dead. His little brother, Irshad, was unaffected but cried incessantly. He was thirteen, his brother three.

He remembered vaguely the trips to market with Baba to sell the handmade furniture and the softness of his mother's hug. They had loved him dearly and he knew it. But Allah had taken them. What had they done to deserve it? It wasn't an honorable death. Even as an adult, the question haunted him.

Irshad was his responsibility and he protected him with heart-felt diligence. Abdul always doted on him, finding ways to acquire candies and things he could use as toys. Even after his uncle came and took Irshad into his home, Abdul continued to look out for his welfare. His brother was his life.

He was driven - from his earliest days in Aldewen to his education in architectural engineering to his legal studies in London and then during the turbulent years of political fighting to make it into Parliament. Twice he had been the country's Foreign Minister and twice he was elected its Prime Minister. He had even hosted an Arab summit conference designed to coordinate strategy against Israel. He recalled with pride how he had been the first Sudanese to speak in the White House and at the UN. As a result, and because of his unique ability to bring together otherwise combative Arab leaders to plot the demise of Israel, he was singularly admired in the Arab world and looked to for leadership behind closed doors.

Abdul did not realize the character changes this brought about. He was blind to the increase in self-importance and gradual desire for more power and notoriety. In spite of this, he was honest and unafraid to ask the difficult questions about everything except his faith. Driven by his understanding of Allah's will, he continued to be considerate and generous. Nevertheless, this same understanding justified ruthlessness when he deemed it necessary. Aliya noticed the changes but loved him too passionately to think less of him.

His first government had been deposed by a radically leftist general and as a consequence he had already spent seven months here in Kober prison, but this time it was different - bloody, violent and without any sense to it. He didn't know who was behind this coup, but it was crystal clear he was going to die soon.

The blasts that shook the prison brought down some of ceiling and opened most of the old cell doors but not Abdul's. Even if it had, he knew it wouldn't matter. He was in the secret part of Kober, that which was never shown to the myriad international agencies. He couldn't escape on his own and all but one of his allies were dead.

Loud bootsteps on the stone floor outside announced the approach of a group of soldiers, but they weren't Sudanese. He could hear them barking out orders to one another with Egyptian accents. Suddenly, the closest door was pushed open and to Abdul's amazement, the very guards who had beaten him mercilessly were dragged into the adjacent cells. Two of them who resisted were shot in the head and left in the hallway.

Suddenly, Abdul feared the worst for his family. Why were Egyptian soldiers killing Sudanese and was he next? He thought to cry out his name but didn't want the spotlight in the midst of this chaos. He wondered if Sudanese independence was over.

He knew that the Egyptians had recently reestablished stronger ties with Russia and had many SVR agents embedded in the military. Abdul was not anti-Russian, but he and his government were strongly independent. Perhaps this was all a ploy to make Sudan a vassal-state subject to the whims of the leftists.

As the faintest glimmer of morning light weaved its way to his cell floor a few hours later, he again heard the Egyptians approach. As they entered, he noticed also Sheikh Dr. Azhari Guma'a, the Grand Mufti of Egypt. Without ceremony, they opened the cell next to Abdul and the Grand Mufti spoke slowly, "You are judged guilty of Fasaad Fi al-Ardh. You have helped spread mischief in the land."

Quickly, a wire noose was placed around the neck of the former guard, now prisoner, and he was hanged there in the cell. His choking lasted several minutes, or so it seemed, during which time the Sheikh peered suspiciously at Abdul.

When the guard finally expired, the Grand Mufti, still staring at Abdul, spoke to the Egyptian soldiers, "Bring him to me."

'This is it', he thought and resolved himself to die with love in his heart for his family and many still undefined questions.

Outskirts of Hillah, Iraq,

Approximately 35 years ago

'There's just no getting rid of him,' he thought. Younger Mahmud adored him, virtually worshipped him and followed him everywhere. He was twelve and Mahmud was only eight. They both lived on the streets, conning or stealing to eat. They knew which market owners were stupid, or so they thought, but one day they got a surprise.

In the market that afternoon was the local Imam who grabbed him roughly by the neck as he was making off with some bread. To his surprise, Mahmud ran up and bit the Imam on the arm making him jerk and yell. Just then, a policeman ran up in response and the Imam began screaming about the "little devils" who had quickly disappeared.

Both of them ran as fast as they could around the back of the market and down a side street until they were out of breath.

"Mahmud, why did you do that? I could have gotten away."

"I'm sorry. I didn't want him to hurt you. You're my best friend."

He was about to punch little Mahmud when he heard more shouting as several people were now chasing them. He pushed him instead, and Mahmud fell to the ground.

Dashing away, he hoped the crowd would just grab his little friend. Each door he tried in the remote alley way was locked until... finally, at the very end, one that opened. Just as he entered, Mahmud appeared behind him out of breath but smiling.

"I thought you were going to leave me!" he whimpered.

"And now you've led them here?!"

"No! No, I hid until they passed and ran around them. They don't know we're here."

He shut the door carefully behind, looking for anyone that may have seen them. They were now on the very outskirts of the city, the surrounding area being rough and rural. A hundred meters away he noticed an old, probably dry well.

"Just shut up Mahmud. We've got nowhere to go if they find us here," he barked.

The little boy backed into the corner and slumped, forlorn that he had disappointed his hero.

The house was dilapidated and mostly fallen down. Rats and feces were abundant. That didn't really matter, they were used to it. So as night fell, they found some cardboard and laid on it.

"Don't get close to me, Mahmud! Go over there near the window," he said forcefully pushing him away.

Mahmud was obedient. The boy flopped down on the dirt floor by the door and was soon asleep. Meanwhile, he devoured the last of the bread they had stolen.

Mahmud had no idea how much he was despised by the person he idolized. He knew his older friend was half Jew and was frequently beaten up by others that knew his heritage. That didn't bother him, after all he was his friend, his only friend.

That night Mahmud slept soundly but his friend did not. The older boy tossed and turned violently and after several hours, jerked upward with sweat dripping down his contorted face. He looked around the room in fear.

"Who are you!?" he whispered loudly. Mahmud did not stir.

"What do you want?" he searched desperately for the presence he knew was there.

There was no sound, nothing audible, but he could see a large dark image across the room approaching him and at the same time sensed screaming, horrible screaming in his mind. The image stood before him for a moment.

"What do you want???" he cried, or at least it seemed like a cry.

At that, the presence came over him, engulfing him. He felt in his mind overwhelming hatred and anger. Then this dark angel hissed, "Kill the boy. Kill the boy and put him in the well."

His angry mind was compliant. In his hand, he found a very old knife, already stained with blood. How did it get there? He didn't know and at the moment didn't care. Below him was Mahmud looking up at him with innocent eyes. There was no conscious thought, only hatred, and the knife plunged deep into the little boy's heart.

As his little friend bled out at his feet, he heard a rooster crow. In almost a mechanical response, he grabbed Mahmud's lifeless body and put him over his shoulder. Silently, he left the house and went to the old well that indeed was dark and dry. The presence said, "Bury him."

He found a rope and tied it off on a post then lowered Mahmud to the bottom. After that, he climbed down the rope to the damp dirt below. With his own hands he scraped and clawed at the dirt for the longest time until there was a hole barely large enough to jam Mahmud's body into and cover it with a few inches of soil.

"I told you to not to get close to me!" he cried at Mahmud.

Slowly, he climbed his way out of the well and to his surprise, there was a small crowd gathered for the morning market. Many noticed him coming out of the well but there were no police. Just as he got out, Mahmud's six-year old brother ran up. Both had been orphans.

"Ismail, you need to come with me," the dark angel whispered in his ear. "Say it!"

"Ismail, you need to come with me," he echoed.

Ismail followed.

Baghdad, Iraq

Over the following years, the presence visited him often teaching him to master deceit and manipulation. As he and Ismail grew, they became increasingly wealthy and corrupt. Unlike Mahmud, Ismail had a heart of stone. By the age of twenty, he took the title of the 'Leader' and had branched out his network to include Riyadh, Amman, and Cairo.

One day they enticed a principle member of the Saudi royal family to join. That was the day the dark angel, now his constant companion, showed him that he had the power to kill just by his thought - something he gleefully used to create submissive associates in more and more cities and governments and to gain unimageable wealth. In the meantime, Ismail proved to be the perfect accomplice – fearful, obedient, and utterly submitted to his master.

Slowly at first, he and Ismail stole to survive. It didn't happen overnight, but it did happen with a supernatural power. As he recognized his calling, they began to trade weapons to al Qaeda and the Kurds. Next, they began to move drugs and desperate people into Europe - all along the way, recruiting associates and finding insidious ways to lure officials into their web. They moved their operational center from Baghdad when the wars came and branched out into Iran, Southern Europe and Russia.

Ismail was diligent in tracking all their assets – people, money and trading goods. After ten years, their network included agents in ten countries and more than two billion euros in reserve. After fifteen, the numbers began to grow exponentially. By twenty, they could pressure governments, corporations and financial institutions very effectively in over fifty major countries and had reserves of nearly three trillion euros held in their own banks all over the world. More than eighteen thousand people had died along the way and those numbers grew as recruits from intelligence agencies joined. Ismail lost a handle on the number of Council associates when it exceeded two hundred thousand and that's when they discovered the power of technology to amplify their control and their reach.

Nevertheless, until the right time, he kept his identity a secret, that is his true identity, which he came to understand, from his 'dark companion', at the age of thirty.

Riyadh, Saudi Arabia

Ibrahim did not have the same latitude of unobserved movement as his 'associates'; as a part of the Royal Family, many if not most of his activities were in the public eye. He still shuddered when he thought of how his heart had stopped beating in the Leader's presence and then started again. The pain and pressure in his chest still shrouded his conscious thought with fear.

He did, however, have his own extensive network of assets especially in northern Africa. The news of the sudden overthrow of Sudan's government meant the potential for serious setback on plans that had been in motion for decades – plans that only he and the top echelon of his clandestine group knew about.

Khartoum wasn't the key; it was the Prime Minister who he needed, and, to his frustration, the radicals had gotten out of the control of his Egyptian partner. Mahgoub could be executed at any time and he had to stop it.

"You cannot allow the PM to be a casualty. Do you understand?" he said forcefully to his aide who nodded and bowed. "Contact the Grand Mufti and use my code. Tell him I want Mahgoub released. He needs to eliminate the threat to the PM but also ensure he is pressured to expatriate. Get it done now! Go!!"

The aide jumped and ran. In minutes, the radicalized usurpers in Khartoum were doomed but Abdul was kept unaware. He had no idea what was happening behind the scenes to move him like a chess piece into a role far more influential than Prime Minister.

Cairo

President Sisi directed the last-minute military campaign to the south from his office. Having learned of the debacle in Khartoum, he decided it was in his best interest to appear as the savior of north African independence and at the same time to eliminate the one serious threat to his own prestige in the Muslim world, Mahgoub.

Within just a few days, the Egyptian army, led by General Berenike, had moved ten thousand troops into position at the border with Sudan. Sisi knew that his own growing relationship with Moscow had opened the door for the overthrow there. He also knew that he would be seen as responsible for turning Egypt into a vassal state of Russia if he did not take this action.

Berenike was the logical choice to carry out the mission, but he was a wildcard with not-too-well hidden ambitions that could be problematic. To engage him in restoring order to the melee in Khartoum would keep him occupied and at 'arms-length' from Cairo.

"General," he spoke into the phone, "we both know the military opposition will be minimal…"

"Yes, Mr. President. Their leadership is in ruins; some on the run, some executed already. There will be no serious push-back," Berenike interrupted with bravado.

"Yes, thank you General. And now if I may finish, your focus must be primarily upon restoring order and setting up an interim government with new leadership. My contacts in Khartoum will deal with the former Prime Minister. Your orders will provide the specifics; you'll have them within the hour. Any questions?"

"No, Sir. It will be done." The General knew Sisi to be dangerous, so for the time being he played the respect card. His pride was consoled by the knowledge that one day the tables would turn.

About an hour later, the orders arrived as promised but Berenike knew he had to stall. It was clear, Sisi wanted not only to take control of

Sudan but to remain in control and to eliminate Mahgoub. The General, however, wanted Sudan for himself and as an associate of Ibrahim, he knew some of what was going on covertly with the PM. Consequently, he felt confident that his status in 'the group' would grow if he could somehow prevent Sisi's plans.

However, before he could make his own move, Sisi sent Russian "advisors" to his command post who effectively took control. In a knee-jerk reaction, Berenike sent a communique to the Saudi Prince which in turn made its way to Tripoli where people he feared far more than Sisi were not pleased.

Tel Aviv

"Go-bag is packed. Teams are mobilized. I'm out of here in five," the Mossad agent sent his encrypted text to Ibrahim. Usually, his missions were all about killing someone; this time, it was a rescue. In a few hours, he had arrived, off-the-books and unknown to the Israeli government, in Khartoum where he and his team found Mahgoub's home surrounded by soldiers. Like a well-trained Seal team, they took out the guards in only a few seconds and entered the house. There they found Aliya and the two children whom they promptly ushered in a less than gentle fashion to their vehicles. In another two hours, they had 'grabbed' Abdul's father-in-law as well and had deposited them all in a well-guarded remote location far south of the city.

"Mama, where is Baba?" Faheemam whimpered to Aliya as they entered the walled compound.

"Sweet one, he is safe, I'm sure, and we must be strong for him," she replied tenderly.

"Will we see him soon, Mama?" added Amani.

"Don't worry, child. Your father is in good hands," the assassin answered.

Faheema was the spitting image of her mother with her long dark Arabic hair and almond shaped eyes. Amani resembled his father – dark skin and a smile that made you laugh, yet with no sense of caution or some would say, common sense. Both children were kind and friendly to everyone they met - a trait that one day would bring unexpected blessings.

Tripoli

Ismael fumed with anger. He had just read Berenike's message to Ibrahim and had conferred with his boss.

"Tell the Israeli to leave his guests in the compound and move Mahgoub to Cairo quickly before Sisi can react. I will take over from there," he texted to Ibrahim.

He packed his bag and holstered his Glock. His irritation with the situation in Khartoum was so bad that he had his aide drive him to the private jet. He had learned to use his anger and not to be controlled by it, but this screw up almost cost them an incalculable loss of time and resource. He could not tolerate it and his boss would most certainly not tolerate it. Soon, he was on his way to Riyadh and then to Cairo.

Chapter 2

Tripoli: Secret Council planning meeting

"Your plan failed in Khartoum!" The hissing whisper rolled off Ismail's tongue like venom.

"The Russians interfered," Baruch retorted. "But we gained an unexpected ally in the process. We'll bring him in soon."

Ismail, who was normally stone cold calm began pacing around the table circling Baruch. He did not look at the General.

"Every piece of the puzzle must fit. We will not tolerate miscalculations. Was it SVR?"

"Yes," grumbled Baruch. "They learned of the overthrow and advised Sisi to clean it up. Berenike was too late to stop it."

A master of military strategy, Israeli General Yosef Baruch was usually in command. Normally, he demanded answers to his own questions. In this circumstance, however, his sharp eyes and fierce countenance were tamed while he rolled a pencil with both hands. Berenike was head of Egypt's Southern Military Region, a Council member with huge influence in Cairo.

"We spent years grooming you and placing you, General." Ismail paused, creating an awkward silence in the dimly lit room. "Are you still confident you can carry out the Council's plans? Or are you uncomfortable? Distracted?"

Ismail was Chief of the Council, 'hand-picked' long ago and sinister enough to thoroughly intimidate the Lieutenant General who ran Israel's elite Shaldag Unit out of Palmachim Airbase. Baruch was supremely a tactician, a masterful one. He was sturdy in build with a short dark beard and commanded some the best warriors in the world. He had earned that role, but long before, he had realigned with the ambitions of the Council, partly for the money, but mostly because he came to believe that the world, starting with the Middle East, was destined to unify, and as one who strove to be in front of his 'destiny', he 'tactically' chose those who would do whatever it took to win. His own people were too fractured, too bent on belonging to the world community, while he wanted to rule it. Meanwhile, he expertly played the role of patriot while his true intent was to extend Israeli dominance far beyond its borders, under his and the Council's guidance that is.

"Who is this unexpected ally?" Ismail queried with a sneer.

"Mahgoub, the Prime Minister. As long as he knows what can happen to his family..." Baruch smiled, "and we have influential people ready to steer him in our direction."

"Yosef, the Leader has already been working on this man for years. Your new ally isn't unexpected, but I congratulate you for your perceptiveness." Ismail almost smiled. "And you're right. We will bring him in soon. As with you, we've been developing him as a key asset."

"Why didn't I know about this?" Baruch was getting agitated. "He might have become collateral. If I am to organize and execute these operations, I need to be informed."

Ismail did not respond.

Education in Sudan is not free. In fact, Abdul struggled to pay for Irshad's primary and secondary schooling. He never considered advancing his own learning as he was destined first for military service. One day, however, his uncle brought the news that he mysteriously was being exempted from service and had received a scholarship to the University in Khartoum. He continuously thanked his uncle, thinking that the old man had paid for everything, something his uncle denied.

He was good at engineering, but his greatest enjoyment was creative and analytical writing. In his senior year, he started a series of poems that glorified Allah and they amazingly got published broadly – in Cairo, Amman, Khartoum and even Riyadh. Shortly after this, he was asked to speak at political rallies and publishers urged him to expand his writing to include his views on the effectiveness of government policies.

Then came the invitation to join the Party and campaign for certain politicians. By that time, Aziz was in the picture and he seemed to know exactly who would win. Abdul had the gift of persuasion and used it marvelously to support the 'right' candidates. Soon, the Party urged him to run for office, as did Aziz and even Aliya. Money poured in from nowhere and his political career took off. As Prime Minister, doors of international influence opened magically and Abdul found himself with grateful allies from Islamabad to Cairo to New York, even D.C. All along, he considered it his good fortune as the blessing of Allah, but this wasn't the case.

Tripoli

Baruch had hoped to place his own puppets in control of Sudan and then Ethiopia to exert additional manipulative control over the African Union as well as a potential roadblock to Saudi domination of the United Muslim world. He wasn't religious; his lust was simply for power and control. The Council's Leader had recognized his potential long ago and certain 'implications' concerning his future were made. But now, he needed to turn his attention to moving forward with the first of the Leader's plans.

Ismail was the only one of the Council who was thoroughly versed with all of them. As the Chief and the Leader's right hand, he did not need to remind Baruch of the consequences of falling short of success. Sudan was important and El-Sisi had his own aspirations, but with Egypt basically in the Council's pocket, he could fix Baruch's snafu. The bigger picture move was still coming and what the General didn't yet know was that Abdul was the critical element. The plans were decades in the making, funded with oil money and tech 'assets' that seemed endless.

"As you know, we're nearly ready for the Iranian move. Within a month Afshin will be running both Quds and Ansar-ul-Mahdi. After that, we can execute the Pasdaran initiative," the General explained with a tinge of hubris.

Afshin was the Council's man in Iran. He had risen through the ranks of the Revolutionary Guard by way of the Council's influence and money. As the head of Quds, he was Iran's main special ops strategist and with the additional responsibility for Ansar-ul-Mahdi, he would control all security for the senior leadership of the government. Baruch had been his handler for the last five years. Before that, it had been Ismail.

Pasdaran is the informal name of the Iranian Revolutionary Guards. The codeword was a reference to the Council's plan to move Ashfin stepwise to the position of commanding all the armed forces of Iran. After that, he would, in conjunction with other plans in motion, ultimately take control of the whole country. In effect, that would lead to dismantling the Shi'ite government.

"A month is too slow. There are a lot of wheels turning. Make it happen in no more than three weeks."

A lot of wheels was an understatement. The Council had its tentacles of influence and control in hundreds of powerful organizations.

"We now basically control the UN General Assembly..." Baruch tried to redeem himself.

"Yes, and our people and assets control enough of the banks, hedge funds, brokerages and government treasuries to swing the major markets as we desire." Ismail replied. "The Assembly will play its part at the right time, but for now our plans for London and Brussels must execute flawlessly. Understood?"

"Will everyone be here tomorrow?" the General shuffled his notes and closed his laptop.

"Be prepared to update on NATO and Pasdaran. No more."

"As you wish."

Tripoli

In the history of the Hebrew people, there were many traitors – Absalom with King David, Judas Iscariot with Jesus, the Jews who profited in Europe by turning their own people over to the Nazis. General Baruch was a club member with VIP standing. His seething scorn for his own people was based in his own incredibly exaggerated self-image. Nothing could satisfy his vanity, and nothing could bridle his ambition.

Every step along the path to command was not simply merited by his natural skill and intellect but accelerated by his talent for eliminating any and all who stood in his way. The Leader saw and appreciated this, even identified, to a certain extent, with it.

Some are formed by life experiences to become monsters Baruch was simply born that way.

As he entered the dimly lit room, he noticed a stink that he loathed. At the large octagonal table in the center sat a single early attendee.

"You still smell like a sewer rat, Amir!" Baruch's voice seemed to mock and jest.

"I've got to stop hanging around your mother," the Iraqi responded with a grunt.

At that, the next two Council members arrived. Berenike and Afshin. They greeted Baruch and Amir with a minimum of formality and sat next to each other on Baruch's right. Amir was a respected member of the Council but its newest and thus its least trusted. As Commander of the Baghdad Operational Command, a Lt. General, he commanded significant forces and he had caught the eye of the Leader during the campaign to eliminate ISIS. With his army initially routed, he was humiliated and broken. That made him a suitable candidate.

The general did indeed have a persistent odor of sweat and cheap cigars. His bravado was a mask for his natural tendency to 'hit and run'. His military command position came by way of a process of elimination – everyone else qualified to lead had been killed. Nevertheless, he adapted quickly to the role and used his excellent survival instincts to recognize opportunity like that offered by the Council and take advantage of it. As for his loyalty, it simply went to the strongest and to the one who could reward him the most.

Of course, both the rise and fall of the so-called ISIS caliphate had all been orchestrated by the Council. Like marionettes, the myriad military groups cooperating against the threat were almost completely manipulated such that, in the process, the Council acquired indescribable wealth. Meanwhile, its power to influence, though entirely clandestine, extended immensely. In addition, Iran and Syria were 'positioned' according the Leader's desire, and Russia ensnared in a noose of Islamic 'relationships' that he planned to use.

'Amir has proven resourceful in this preparation for Phase Two,' Baruch mused. He pondered the other two. Afshin was dangerous but committed. Normally, a contingent of Quds bodyguards traveled with him, but not now.

The Council's gatherings were far beyond confidential and secretive. Baruch recalled three members who had been 'sanctioned' for simple but unforgivable mistakes in personal security. At nearly 190 cm, Afshin was unusually tall for an Iranian from Shiraz. He was highly trained and effective in killing. He was also a capable strategist. If he had a weakness, Baruch didn't know it.

Ashfin was a cat. Intelligent to be sure, but also patient in the hunt. He joined the military not for idealistic reasons but simply to survive the chaos of Iran's economy and xenophobic society especially in his home region in the south. His physique made is easy for him to stand out during training and those around him looked up to him not just literally but in admiration as well. He knew how to make alliances.

He was a natural leader which led to quick progression up the ranks. When he caught the eye of the Leader, he was ready to hunt the greatest quarry, Israel and to lead the new Persian empire.

Then there was Berenike - a snake with a no qualms of who he was loyal to - the Leader.

But before he could finish the mental assessment of his audience, the Prince arrived. Dressed as an ordinary Libyan, but with an unmistakable countenance of authority, the Saudi sat at the table without so much as a nod. Folding his hands, he looked impatiently at Baruch.

"Ten minutes," he said matter-of-factly. Everyone understood the time constraint. More than anyone else, members of the Saudi royal family were under a microscope. Extraordinary precautions had to be made for him to be present even for that short time. Normally, all engagement with him was handled by Ismail in Riyadh or in the air. Today, the Leader required an in-person consensus of Baruch's proposal.

Ismail entered next and glared at the remaining empty seat.

"Begin! And shut the door," he barked.

As the door was closing, finally, the last and most valuable member arrived.

Cairo, three days earlier

As steam from the cup swirled upward, Abdul sipped his coffee at the outside table. His nerves were still on edge. Back in Kober's sub-basement, the Sheik had grilled him for hours. He wasn't tortured, but he was convinced that the order for his execution could come at any moment. Would he answer honestly? Was he responsible for the insurrection? Why was he in prison? Did he want to consolidate his own power?

And then the questions on Islam; What did he really believe? Are there any other gods besides Allah? Could he recite the pillars? What were his 'last days' views? Was he supportive of a world-wide Muslim Union?

For hours and hours, it continued. Many of the inquiries surprised him? He was, after all, a well-recognized Islamic writer and had mused upon some of the topics, but eschatology questions in a prison? Could he work with Shiites?

Then, as though on a schedule, the Sheik had departed, and he was roughly ushered to the prison exit. Outside, was his father-in-law, who also gave Abdul a piercing glare, then put his arm around him.

"You must put yourself in exile for some time, my son. This country is too unstable at present and your presence is dangerous for my children." Aziz had spoken firmly.

"Go to Cairo. Here's the address where you will be contacted and some money for the trip. Don't worry, I will take care of the family, but you must go now! Do not go home."

Presently, in this busy bazaar-type alley of the Egyptian capital with its merchants and crowds, as he finished the sweet coffee, avoiding the grounds, the thought struck him, 'Had he been 'vetted'?? Was his detention not about the fall of his government but rather something else? Crazy idea!'

The busy walkway outside the El Fishawi cafe was lined on both sides with little tables. Each pair of adjacent tables could accommodate four. Abdul sat on the outside wondering if he would have to make a quick escape. He knew the large number of diners and shoppers in the small street would be helpful cover... maybe. 'Who was coming? More than one person? Was this a set up to simply eliminate him outside his own country? Surely not in such a public place.'

The blue and yellow light bulbs hanging across the narrow alley reflected upon the decorative glass hanging lamps below as well as the ornate brassware. Across from him was a shop with glass-cased shelves crowded with multicolored glassware and ceramics. In the distance a red and green neon sign hung over the entrance to a pipe shop while leather slippers and bluish fabric of all kinds were displayed on both sides. Shop owners who stood waiting to entice passersby to consider their merchandise were momentarily amusing. Looking up, he saw that the café's outdoor tables were sheltered under a loose green fabric covering overhead.

Inside, thick sweet coffee and tea were served along with plastic bottles of Dasani or Aquafina water. Some enjoyed a platter of pumpkin and sunflower seeds as well. Hookah pipes rested on stands by the tables. It was all familiar to him a for a brief moment, he felt relieved.

As he wrestled with his anxiety, a small group passed by, and in a blink his table was suddenly shared with another man. Abdul nearly swallowed the grounds in his cup - a Jew?!

Tripoli

Just as the door was closing, in came Yehuda, a bit out of breath. He nodded to Ismail and Baruch but appeared disinterested in the others. He clearly understood his value and standing with the Council which had been established over a long tenure. You don't rise through the ranks of Mossad quickly or without extreme scrutiny and he had mastered that patient subterfuge.

Yehuda Cohen's connections world-wide alone made him perhaps the most powerful manipulator, next to the Leader, of any intelligence agent or politician. At least that was his own assessment. On top of that, he had logged more assassinations personally than any member of his Kidon unit.

At first, his 'wetwork' had been all about patriotism. But eventually, it had turned him apostate both religiously and toward his country.

Growing up in Gush Etzion Junction, Yehuda was close to many people, friends and family who were abducted, tortured, even beheaded. Reputed to be the most dangerous place in Israel, it was the perfect place for a young man to become hardhearted and ruthless. He survived by being more violent than the attackers and developing his own gangs to administer retribution.

He honed his skills during his military service and went straight into Mossad afterward. Despite the barrage of patriotism displayed around him, he never became 'infected' with it. His only goal was to become the most proficient assassin in the directorate. He never flinched when killing - old, young, men, women – it was basically sport and often tickled his rotten heart with excitement.

Ismail encountered him in Kabul and recognized his potential to serve the Council. They were both after the same target and as a result nearly killed each other but made peace after a stalemate. Soon, he was introduced to the Leader who 'adjusted' the killer's heart and gained his loyalty.

At the present time, his ambitions were simply about wealth and power. He had already accrued nearly as much personal treasure as the Prince in conjunction with his murders, but the wealth only burned inside him. Not so secretly, he considered himself more astute and capable than anyone else in the room, perhaps anyone period.

"OK, now that we are all here… Baruch, please begin and be brief," Ismail directed.

"Quickly… since Amir's guards are clearly anxious…" interjected Yehuda, grinning slightly.

"How did you spot them?!" interjected the Saudi Prince. Amir just frowned.

Yehuda peered back. "Really?"

"Anyway, mission accomplished in Cairo. I'll tell you more after Baruch," he teased.

Baruch began with London. "Khan has successfully recruited a high-level team in the London Stock Exchange Group and thus can maneuver Borsa Italiana, Russell, and several other exchanges." He continued with a few of the financial initiatives he had worked on with the politician.

Abdu Kahn was slick. He was a financial genius and used his talent to build connections in the London financial world. Amassing his own personal wealth of over two billion euros via market manipulation and blackmail, he accidentally ran a Ponzi scheme on Ismail who likewise was slick. Ismail reacted by planning to kill him, but the Leader decided to use Kahn's skills to establish the Council's own complete world-wide financial system not unlike the dark web compared to the internet.

To ensure Kahn's façade was credible throughout Europe, the Council used its influence to get him into the position of Mayor of London. A position he used craftily to enhance the Council's financial agenda.

After he discussed the status of the bloc of control they now possessed in the UN, he turned to Phase One of the NATO/EU plan.

"I'll finish with the one proposal we need consensus on. Each of you has discussed this in detail with me individually. NATO must be transitioned into the EU military. I won't reiterate the operational details but by the time this happens, our Muslim Union will control from Morocco to Indonesia. Phase Two will include the US and ultimately it will be the alliance between the three which will provide an overwhelming world-wide force under our control. We've already prompted our senior political assets in France and Germany to 'study' this transition and publicly advocate it."

"And I have already committed resources to support this including the major European media players," added the Prince.

"Currently, I see three, perhaps four significant obstacles to eliminate at the top level politically and we will be ready to address them, with the Leader's approval, of course," offered Cohen.

"And speaking of media, we all know our greatest successes have been underscored by our existing media control, providing continuous propaganda – that, along with our comprehensive communication plans. Along that line, although the SVR caused a wrinkle in Baruch's Khartoum project...," Baruch didn't react, "my meeting in Cairo has brought us someone truly gifted in crafting and disseminating the new message."

"I think I know who you are referring to," chimed in Berenike, "but is he really the one?"

"More to determine on that, but he has been initially screened and actually, we've secretly prepped him for most of his life," answered Yehuda.

"OK, I take it by your comments that you all indeed support the NATO or 'N-plan'. We'll call it that from now on," Baruch finished.

The Prince stood, nodded and left the room.

"Is there any disagreement or lack of clarity on our ultimate goal in Europe or your individual deliverables?" Ismail seemed to discourage any questions with his tone.

"Good. You are each responsible for your standing missions as well as the new program. You'll cooperate fully with Cohen on this. He and Baruch will complete the operational strategies and report to me. Understood?"

The Council adjourned, and each member disappeared into the dark of Tripoli's evening.

Chapter 3

Cairo

His meeting with this Jew, Yehuda, left Abdul somewhat aghast. Now, he found himself looking over his shoulder every minute or so.

They had only been talking for a couple of minutes when a small bomb exploded inside the cafe. Both of them got up from the street shaking off glass shards and debris. Then quickly, the Mossad assassin had grabbed Abdul by the arm and dragged him to the inside of another shop some 50 meters down the street. A moment afterward, they were shown a small back room with a rear exit.

"That wasn't supposed to happen! El-Sisi wants you out of the way. Your clout is a threat to his own pitiful ambitions," Yehuda had murmured to him.

"But we're safe here for a short while. As I was saying, I know some people who are interested in your talents for communication, for speaking, writing and expertly crafting any message you intend. As a matter of fact, they have been observing for quite a long time and have secretly invested in you - your university scholarships, your political rise, even your literary notoriety."

"Who are these people?!" exclaimed Abdul, still catching his breath.

"Not so loud. You don't need to know just yet. That will come. First, you do need to know that the overthrow in Khartoum was actually due in part to our interest, and unfortunately there are powerful organizations, rivals if you would, that have learned about it. They will likely try to suck you into their own plans. The Egyptian president, as I said, just wants you dead."

"Abdel? That's hard to believe! I've known him since the Egyptian Command and Staff College internship years ago."

"He is not the same man. Publicly, he is polished and has become a statesman of sorts. In reality, his goals interfere with those of my friends. We will deal with him at the right time," said the Jew.

"But what do your friends want from me?!" Abdul was agitated and scared.

"I'll meet with you again in a few days and explain more. Abdul, trust me, you don't know how lucky you are. However, you will have to be circumspect and very careful. Don't return to your hotel. Here's some money. Get a room at the Royal Maxim Palace. Shave your facial hair and dress like a European. We'll hide you in plain sight."

"Can I see my family? I had to leave so quickly..."

"Of course. But not immediately. In the short term, I will have some of my assets keep an eye on you, but you won't see them." Yehuda used his phone to give someone a one-word code and ended the call.

"Abdul, understand that everything for you up to this point has actually been preparation. You have an amazing future in front of you that will far surpass your wildest dreams. Can I count on you to keep an open mind?"

"I don't even know your name, how can I..."

"Call me Yehuda. It's not my real name but that's what I'm called."

"Ok, I'll try but honestly, it's all a bit overwhelming."

"Good. I'll reconnect in three days."

"Where? When exactly?"

"Don't worry. I'll find you. Now, exit through this back door and go straight to the Royal and do NOT contact your family yet. Understood?"

With that, Yehuda had departed. Now, as Abdul approached the turn-off from el Sadat Street, he could see the hotel just off highway six. On the way, he had noticed at least a couple of men he thought might be following him. As Yehuda told him, his face and head were now shaven, and the new 'European' cloths were too tight, but the cafe bomb had shaken him enough that he felt like he should take the stranger's advice.

As he crossed the street, he was startled by a speeding van that seemed headed straight for him. But, before it could reach him or he could jump out of the way, another car came out of nowhere and rammed into it on the driver's side, clearly killing whoever was in it. Immediately, the driver of the car jumped out, took a quick look in the van and as sirens began to whine, sped away on foot.

Cairo

The elaborate Royal Suite was a world away from his cell in Kobers. Abdul drew the heavy cream- colored drapes closed and sat on the soft sofa facing the ornate over-sized coffee table.

The Kempinski or as it is known locally, the Royal, is as high end as it gets in Cairo. The Royal Suite redefined plush, having its own bedroom, dining room, living room, and exercise area. As Abdul, wandered through it, he noticed the entire bedroom was gilded – gold curtains, gold walls, gold bed, gold lamps and desks, even the myriad picture frames on the walls were gold, not paint – gold.

Next, was the dining room with eight padded chairs covered with shimmering silver fabric surrounding a large teak table. The expansive living room also sported gold-trimmed furniture, four separate seating areas a massive chandelier and a wide vista of the city. Finally, the bath room was futuristic and fit for a king.

Abdul was assigned a 24-hour butler, spa service, a private lounge on the third floor and even a fitness coach.

On the table in front of him was a cardinal red envelope with a seal having an odd emblem. It was labeled simply A. Mahgoub - read now. As he reached to open it, he was startled by a sharp rap upon the door. Again, the rap, but harder.

"Khidmat alghuraf!"

Abdul had not ordered any room service so he approached the door carefully wishing he had something he could use to defend himself. As he peered through the security hole, he could see what appeared to be a serving cart with a large covered silver platter. He shook himself and slowly opened the door.

There was no one with the cart but to his surprise, two formally dressed men, each with a beard, stood on either side of the entrance. They acknowledged him but did not speak. The slight bulge under their suit-coats indicated they were armed. A simple hand motion from one of them made it clear that Abdul should take the cart into the room.

Rolling it inside, he found under the cover a Jericho 941 polymer pistol with two 9x19 cartridges and a note. It simply read, "Use only in extreme emergency. Yehuda"

He recognized the Israeli handgun, having procured one himself during his first term as Prime Minister.

Abdul shook his head, 'He seems to think of everything.'

Sitting back on the sofa, he opened the seal on the envelope and began reading the lengthy missive it contained. Beforehand, he noted that it was signed by several Arab heads of state and/or their defense ministers each of whom he knew well. They eloquently expressed their support for him and though they were diplomatic in their wording, it was clear they were upset with the Egyptian President for his role in Abdul's exile.

They concluded with, "We remember with appreciation your masterful facilitation of our Arab League Summit meetings in Dhahran and esteem you as the rightful leader of Sudan. Our Foreign Ministers will continue to include you."

Cairo

The next two days passed without incident. The two guards disappeared from the door, but Abdul had the distinct sense that they were still nearby. He cautiously used the hotel's indoor pool and spa, keeping his firearm close and struggling mentally with not being able to contact anyone.

For better or worse, the time was a respite allowing him to ponder his situation. Abdul was a passionate man. His heart ached for Aliya and the children while in contrast, he determined to destroy those who had attacked him and endangered them.

He didn't feel safe, but he felt safer. Sinking into the soft cushions of one of the chairs he began to reflect upon the chaos in his country and his part in it all. All the way back to his beginnings with the Umma Party, he was a radical – young, thinking he knew everything and could singlehandedly save his homeland from the problems it faced. Aggression from Egypt, anger in the South, attempted coups from the Communists, poverty, government fraud and corruption, disastrous handling of the cotton crops, the list scrolled through his mind like an old movie.

He spent several times in prison along the way, counting on Allah's mercy. Then came Aliya and he began to grow up. No longer was it all about him, making his mark, saving the day alone. Helping his country to emerge from catastrophe and turmoil was also about making it safe for his loved ones.

Then came the anxious thoughts. What had he done?! Where was his country headed now?? Where was his faith in all of this? Was he really the Amallah others thought him to be?

And where was he headed? Should he simply face the acute danger of returning to Khartoum? Would Aziz really be able to protect Aliya and the children? Perhaps he should turn to his friends in Riyadh or Amman or even here in Cairo. Who could he trust and who might simply take him for ransom?

On the morning of the third day, Yehuda met him at a table near the outdoor pool along with another stranger, possibly a Saudi. Both of them seemed very much at ease in contrast to how Abdul felt.

"The incident outside the hotel when you arrived probably caught you off-guard," Yehuda began. "It was an assassin from Khartoum. We were notified in advance of it by one of our friends whom you know quite well, Aziz."

"Aziz works with you!?" Abdul let it slip out with more surprise than he intended.

"Not exactly. Let's just say he's a friend," Yehuda responded coolly.

"Abdul, let me introduce you to Ibrahim. He is a man of considerable resource and wants to help us help you."

They nodded to one another, though Abdul was now skeptical of both these men. He instantly recognized the Prince of course and instantly wondered as well why the younger relative of his friend Prince Abdulaziz bin Turka Al Saud, a great sports enthusiast, was accompanying the Jew.

"Prince, I am honored to meet you. How is Abdulaziz?" he asked.

"He is well. Still promoting Formula One racing fanatically. Inshallah, we will become good friends as well, Mr. Mahgoub," Ibrahim assured him.

"A worthy cause makes worthy friends," added Yehuda.

"But Abdul, we must provide you some direction and friendly advice. We have arranged for you to spend some time in London and Brussels. Your accommodations and financial resources have been established. Are you ready to do some 'study'?"

"More schooling?"

"Perhaps. If you want to think of it that way. However, our intent is that you develop your already excellent skills to learn the most effective ways of... let's say communicating convincingly with the western mind – learn how they think and what they respond to emotionally."

"All right, but what will we communicate?"

"Well, many things, and some very similar to what you have already published but perhaps with a small twist."

The Saudi chimed in, "I will open doors for you, Abdul, to establish strong ties with those in the European Media Alliance and Sky."

"One year in London. One year in Brussels. Throughout that time and afterwards, we'll assess your progress." Yehuda was straight to the point. "Ibrahim will pass messages from you safely to your family through Aziz. And as I mentioned previously, my men will look out for you, covertly. You will leave Cairo tomorrow. Don't worry, I'll stay in contact with you via secure text," he handed a cell to Abdul.

"And needless to say, do not tell anyone about us or the nature of your activities; that would have very dire consequences. Do you understand?"

"Of course," he replied but was surprised it came out so calmly. Inside, he was still spinning with confusion and anger about the crazy turn his life had taken over the last week. 'What is this message? Why were a Jew and a Saudi cooperating and offering him help? Why the time-line of two years? Did that coincide with something else?' Abdul had a tendency to question everything even in normal times but now his mind raced with hyper-inquisitively.

Isleworth, UK

Sky CEO Dirroch who also reported to the parent company Comcase was placed in his position by the Council as were Griffins, Conyer, Davet, Klien, Roolen, and Schmid. The recent Comcase purchase, being underwritten by a bank owned by the Council ensured adherence to directives received from the secretive group. This particular meeting had a visitor from Libya at the table, Ismael.

The guest began, "We are moving one of our senior assets here to work with you and the European Media Alliance to present social content and a new spin on world events that embraces international harmony. You will consider him for the time being as a direct connection with your boss's boss's boss. I hope that is clear. He will work directly with you, all your divisions and with other media companies to promote a new and compelling communication strategy. Ms Klien, you will be expected to align all marketing with the new theme and each of you shall drive it down into the editorial and especially the entertainment divisions."

Ismail did not sugar-coat anything. He knew Abdul had the talent to be effective in his new role, but he wanted to ensure there would be no quibbling.

"You are also to keep PM Mahgoub's role very, very low key. You may speak of him only as an advisor."

At the mention of Abdul, eyebrows raised across the room.

"Sir," queried Davet, "the UK has a unique way of interpreting what is presented in the media. Is a Sudanese really going to be able to communicate fluidly with us, I mean with the British people?"

Ismail's eyes grew red with ire and he stood up at the table. He glared at Davet and then the rest of the group. "We will address your concerns, Mr. Davet, after the meeting," he said slowly enough to drive home his intentions. Then he looked at Dirroch with a serious frown and nodded.

"This meeting is over," the CEO said tersely. "Let's get on with it."

Later that evening, Mr. Davet tragically experienced a fatal car accident on the way home. He was replaced quickly with a man from the Middle East.

Sky News operated, as a joint venture, the sister channel Sky News Arabia via the Abu Dhabi Media Investment Group. Conveniently, it was a Council investment and allowed easy two-way interaction for Abdul's message strategy to propagate into both the Middle East and the EU. The Comcase linkage to NBC also made a convenient pathway for the strategy in the US.

London

The City, as it is called, occupies about a square mile of downtown and is the first of two major financial districts in the British capital. HSBC, Barclay's, Lloyd's and several others represented the hub of financial activity in the EU. Each had board members loyal to the Council and to Khan, the Council's senior financial agent in Europe.

Ismail, Ibrahim and the former Mayor of the city pulled together a secret meeting of the CEOs of these institutions. The secrecy was not at all unusual, but the 'request' was extraordinary. After the initial shock and twenty minutes of discussion, there was a wrap-up.

"All right, in summary, together you are secretly holding more than six trillion of the Council's assets. We'll give you thirty days to shuffle your accounts and send the 800 billion we are withdrawing to the designated financial agency in Rome," said Khan smoothly.

"The ECB and World Bank are to know absolutely nothing about this. If there are any leaks, I will plug them myself," added Ismail sternly.

"And we were never here!" added Ibrahim.

The CEOs wisely remained silent and after looking at each other, simply nodded.

London

Abdul arrived at Heathrow in the midst of a security alert. Consequently, it took him nearly two hours to reach the cab. Once settled in his new home in the posh St. Edmunds Terrace, he scribbled out a text he intended to send to the family via Ibrahim. Looking around the eight million dollar house (or so it had been estimated by the driver) he thought, 'If this is any indication, they must have plenty of resources available and some very serious intentions.'

His first assignment from Ismail was to draft a speech for the Saudi Ambassador to the UN and to meet with the COO/CFO of Sky Group at the Isleworth Centre. There was no problem getting the meeting within just a few days which impressed him.

The topic of the speech was unexpected as well; "regional and global stability through common goals." Instead of another thrashing of Israel or spotlighting again the plight of Gaza, the focus was to be upon the noble cause of a united Muslim world through constructive dialog on differences.

In addition, he began working with senior contacts at SkyNews to develop a promotion of this theme across Europe and the Middle East. Over the next month, he wrote several more speeches and met clandestinely with news editors in order to plan a campaign of 'cultural awareness' across the EU and the US. News programs and entertainment series all embraced Abdul's 'message' seemingly for the sake of promoting open peaceful societies. It became so pervasive and effective that radio, internet and even commercial marketing firms picked it up. The receptivity utterly amazed Abdul. Actually, it seemed too good, even supernatural, and that scared him.

Abdul was able to renew the Sky News resource-sharing agreement with CBS News in the US much to the chagrin of the BBC who acknowledged that because of Abdul's work Sky News was the first choice for "key opinion formers."

His office was in the newer Studio 21 facility from where he managed the negotiations in the Netflix partnership with Sky and gave 'advice' to senior editorial and media directors.

At Ismail's direction, Abdul began to consult with EU leadership including select leaders in many European countries, especially France and Germany. Horst Seehofen, German Minister of the Interior, Dr. Markus Richtenhof, Vice President of BAMF and Benjamin Grivee, Socialist and Government Spokesperson for France all became close confidants and as Council assets, opened doors for broad influence.

Many of the Council's goals depended upon the acceptance of large influx of immigrants into Europe who helped to alter traditional perceptions and ultimately, values.

After a year of this experience or 'study' as Yehuda called it, he could spin a storyline, a message, any message really, to appear completely natural, compelling and logical for westerners to accept. At the same time, he had witnessed the control his new 'friends' were exerting to a greater and greater degree over the financial centers of London. On the anniversary of his assignment, Ismail visited.

Having never studied psychology, Abdul started his study of the western mind with a clean slate. His African perception was mixed with his Muslim ideals and gave him a somewhat jaded opinion of many things western, but he was irked by the obsession with self, self-importance, self-gratification and self-centeredness. He learned how easily the western mind could be manipulated by the fear of rejection and peer pressure. He saw an already decaying value system torn apart by the relentless pursuit of pleasure and was aghast at the universal apathy which seemed to be born out of too much – too much of everything. He learned quickly just how much unearned credibility the media had to westerners. They never really questioned it – if it was in print, it must be true.

All of these things, he was able to incorporate into a propaganda or rather message strategy that became extremely effective. Much of the groundwork had already been done by the eroding cultures he sought to influence.

The doorbell rang and surprised Abdul. He strangely shivered and suddenly felt chilled.

"Ismail, welcome, come in. May I bring some tea?" he was relieved to see a somewhat familiar face. Over the course the last year, they had corresponded frequently.

"Yes, that would be fine. Are we alone?"

"Oh yes." Abdul fumbled a bit with the sugar.

"My friend, it seems like you have exceeded the progress we hoped for and the Leader is pleased."

"Ismail, I thought you were the Leader..."

"Good tea," he interrupted and paused with a sullen frown. "However, I bring you not only news of our satisfaction but also a warning. I've learned that you may be approached by the SVR. They have noticed the swing in public sentiment throughout the EU in favor of our message as opposed to the downturn in excitement about socialism and they are envious so to speak. Of course, Yehuda can run in front of that, but be aware of the threat."

Abdul was a pragmatist. He saw some of the 'noble' aspects of socialism but also, from personal experience and from diligent study, was well aware of its repeated failures. He recognized that it could never really work simply because of the same things he had observed in the western mind. That was why 'socialist' governments inevitably nurtured a corrupt elite at the top and an impoverished servant class below. It was the perfect environment for totalitarianism which he saw as either good or bad depending on the culture.

He knew that for decades, the powers that be from former communist states had patiently strived to infiltrate the myriad systems of the west with socialist tenets – schools, media, judicial and even legislative systems became increasingly shaped to support their doctrine.

The Council's message, on the other hand, acknowledged the supreme need for humans to be unified and that all governments, faiths, cultures would find a perfect world in this unity.

As the Libyan spoke, Abdul noticed for the first time a subtle but distinct 'darkness' that had settled in the sitting room. Maybe it was just Ismail's mood. He started to get up and open the partially drawn curtains. Ismail looked at him in the eye and slowly shook his head after which Abdul carefully took his seat again. Not only that, but he felt this great sense of foreboding and fear.

"You've noticed the power behind this message, haven't you?" Ismail continued with a very slightly sinister grin. "You should embrace that power, Abdul. The other parts of our plans are proceeding nicely and will culminate with the next major phase if you are as successful in Brussels. Have you prepared for that?"

He did not know as yet what the 'next phase' was to be, but his UN contacts had paved the way for him to become a Special Consultant to the EU President on Muslim and Middle East affairs.

"I believe so. I'm positioned and prepared to steer the EU to support the Muslim Union."

Ismail smiled. Standing to leave, he noticed the letter from the heads of state that Abdul had received in Cairo. It was modestly framed and hanging on the wall to encourage the former PM.

"I thought you would appreciate that," he said, with a subtle wink.

"How did you... You mean... ??" Abdul just then began to grasp the influence Ismail had at the highest levels.

Brussels

For all his adult life, Abdul had felt that his accomplishments, his rapport in the Arab world and in the West were of his own making - his wits, his talents, his je ne sais quoi, but as they traveled to Brussels, Ismail elaborated with convincing detail how the "Council" had arranged nearly all of it. Abdul was floored, then dismally discouraged, then thoroughly intimidated. Ismail enjoyed watching these reactions and seemed to know exactly what to say and when, to reel him up as he was emotionally crashing - just as if he had done it many times before.

"So, what's the history behind the "Council"? Who is on it?" Of course, as usual, Abdul had too many questions.

"If Allah wills it, you will get all your answers, Abdul. Now, before we begin this next episode of your studies, how is your family doing?" This he said knowing all supposed messages from his family were falsified and contrived to manipulate Abdul. "I understand Aziz was seriously hurt just recently."

"Aziz hurt?! I didn't know that! What happened?"

"Oh, it seems he was mugged by some dangerous people on his way home from prayers. You know, as I said before, he is indeed a friend of ours and has been for many years, but even friends sometimes have to learn from mistakes."

After that, both men were silent for the rest of the trip, but Abdul strongly suspected that Aziz's 'mistakes' and 'lessons learned' had something to do with the "Council". In any event, he didn't dare to allow himself more questions.

Upon arriving at Brussels Airport, they made their way to a standing limo and began to get in when Ismail took a call. He seemed unusually agitated and immediately excused himself. He dashed back into the terminal and no sooner had he left than, to Abdul's amazement, Irshad, his younger brother appeared, out of breath.

"Abdul, Aziz sent me to warn you..." he blurted out even before a handshake.

Suddenly, a shot rang out, muffled by the airport traffic. Irshad's chest blew open with blood covering Abdul and he dropped to the pavement dead. Abdul was in shock and stood motionless until the limo driver pushed him into the car and sped off.

"Wait!! Wait! That's my brother! You can't just leave him!"

"I have to get you to safety," the driver said slightly nervous but remarkably more calm than Abdul would have expected. "Our people will see to him shortly. I'm so very sorry for your loss."

It had happened so fast... and where was Ismail?! What did he mean "warn you"? Irshad had been in university in Paris and how did he know to find him here and now?? 'Dear, dear brother, how can I...' his mind raced, shuffling between grief, guilt and anger.

"Who did this??!!" he cried.

Chapter 4

Barcelona, three years ago

The train ride from the 'castle' into the city took about thirty minutes. As it was early in the morning there were few passengers, so James found himself daydreaming while watching the countryside pass by. The estate that they were allowed to use as caretakers was indeed like a castle. It looked like something out of a travel magazine. Being very old, there were no modern conveniences apart from the cold-water shower and ancient toilets. The kitchen had an antique stove and an open wood hearth. Even the hallways upstairs displayed suits of armor from knights of old. Nevertheless, he and Vanessa were thankful to have use of it.

He thought again about how they met just one year ago. It was a music festival in England. He caught sight of her walking with some friends and instantly he was enchanted. He could never figure why she would even give someone like him the time of day. Her eyes sparkled. She laughed so genuinely and when he approached her, some kind of switch somewhere flipped on because they both knew instantly they had a future together.

Only a few days after they met, she and her friends invited him to a gathering, a party of sorts, where they both became interested in an ongoing discussion on some pretty deep topics. 'Too deep for me,' he had thought initially, but when he noticed Vanessa tuning in, he listened closer. In a few minutes, or so it seemed, he was truly engaged himself in the conversation.

"But how can I know, really know, that what you're claiming is true?" was his final inquiry.

"You can't simply figure it out, James. It is a surrender in your heart. Ask Him to show you, and He will. Then ask Him to forgive you, and He will. Then ask Him to teach you, and He will."

Seemed simple enough, but he still wanted to think on it, to break it down and despite the tug on his heart, to see if he could dismiss it.

Didn't work that way though. By evening, back home on the edge of his bed, he sat struggling in his mind. Finally, he opened his heart and that night slept like a new born babe. The next day, he found that Vanessa had had a similar experience. A few months later, we were married.

Of course, that didn't happen overnight. There were romantic dinners in Little Venice, exploring the Columbia Road flower market together where James learned that color meant more to Vanessa – blue – than the type of flower, and a lovely scent to be sure. They picnicked frequently on Primrose Hill on the north side of Regent Park overlooking London where Vanessa learned James could not make a decent potato salad to save his life.

"You're always wearing a blue flower in your hair, why a yellow one today?" James asked and prided himself for being so observant.

"Oh, I'm just expanding my horizons I guess," she responded with a smile that was an invitation for a kiss. She knew that yellow was his favorite color.

She melted into his arms and just then little Michael rushed up.

"Daddy, can we fly a kite like those other people??"

They all laughed at the innocence of the interruption and both roared, "Yeah, let's do it!" So, the romantic kiss had to wait.

However, over the course of five to six months they fell deeper and deeper in love. Then, on a beautiful sunny day in June, under the leafy lovers' arch in the Kensington Palace gardens, James came through and made Vanessa a proposal that brought her tears of joy and a shout to the whole world, "Yes, Yes!"

Now, for both of them, sharing the reality of divine love was a key part of their lives. As an artist, James was a capable illustrator while Vanessa was a math whiz. Together, they were able to make ends meet and have time to work with various charities.

The train jarred against the track and brought him back to the 'real world'. As it did, he noticed the sunrise and somehow, along with the day, the sudden realization dawned on him as well that his beautiful wife was pregnant. Sure enough, nine months later, in a farm house outside Toledo, Spain, Tasha was born.

The bump in the road, so to speak, was their families. Vanessa was Jewish and her parents were angry that James was not. Of course, they were even more distraught with Vanessa's new faith.

After the craziness of his first marriage, James never imagined being happy again. Shortly after his little brother had died, when he and his whole family were grieving, 'she' came around and latched on to James. She was a good actor and played the role well before family and friends but not long after their union, she began making excuses for taking 'girl time' in the evenings. She got pregnant and James always assumed the baby was his but after the boy was born and only two years old, she simply left them both with no word. A year later, she popped back into their lives and tried to get sole custody of Michael but failed.

All that seemed like a lifetime ago and James forced the painful memories to become lessons learned. Vanessa couldn't imagine a girl leaving him – handsome, kind, strong and yet so thoughtful. And she loved Michael intensely.

James' parents wanted him to annul the new marriage. However, neither one of them ever doubted for a minute the love they shared or the course of their life together. In fact, long walks together, hand in hand, made every evening seem almost like a dream and the Barcelona promenade magical.

James also had a gift for languages and that made it possible for him to join a translation firm. His role was to establish the translating teams and ensure the process they used produced a high quality of work. The company acknowledged his efforts in Spain and soon they were doing the same thing in Paris and then Hamburg. Finally, he was sent to Athens. As he considered the ensuing lifestyle - low pay, lots of moves but exposure to lots of interesting people to share with – he always gave thanks for the love of his life and her willingness to be his partner in it all.

Vanessa could have been a concert violinist; she could have been a CFO. She was amazingly gifted in design. But her greatest gift was motherhood. Her child benefited by a constant stream of love, love that sacrificed and yet sang sweetly, love that searched for ways to comfort and bless. She loved James passionately and she loved her child perfectly.

Athens

In the tiny bedroom of their rented house in Penteli outside Athens, James sat on the edge of the bed with their newborn son on his lap. His wife, Vanessa was nearby in the next room when suddenly, the little baby turned blue and stopped breathing. In shock, James frantically called out to her and started gently breathing into the child's mouth. After a few breaths, the baby began to weakly inhale and exhale again, but remained blue.

As quickly as possible, they raced to the nearest hospital, praying and in tears. A few hours later, little John Lance was in the pediatric critical care unit with tubes and drip lines and what seemed like a freakish amount of medical equipment hooked up to him.

James and Vanessa were desperately looking for answers and help in their faith. At first, the doctors were unsure what the problem was as their tests only revealed an infection, but later they determined the cause and arrived at the diagnosis of septicemia with meningitis. Sadly, the hospital did not have the proper medicines nor doctors with the experience necessary to help. For weeks, the parents had the painful ordeal of watching their little one continue to weaken and finally pass away.

Married only a few years, they had come to Greece with the intent to simply help people who were down and out or despondent, with the faith and hope they themselves had experienced. After the death of their child, it was consequently they who needed someone with a kind heart to minister to them. They were crushed in spirit and hurting as only someone who has lost a child can hurt. Friends couldn't help. Counselors seemed shallow.

For a while, each day was seemingly filled with meaninglessness; each night with tears. However, months passed and slowly they began to want to get back to their original intentions.

James worked tirelessly with a translation and printing business; however, needing to earn some more income to make ends meet, he would take his guitar and play at myriad outdoor cafes during the evenings.

One night, as he and Vanessa were headed home after a long evening, a man sitting at an outdoor cafe table waved vigorously and called for them to come over and sing a song. Now, the table was also occupied by eight or nine very large and 'serious-looking' men along with the man who had beckoned them. Looking friendly but dignified, he sat at the far end.

James looked at Vanessa and said, "You better stay here. If you see anything getting out of hand, run and call for an astynomikos."

She grabbed his arm, "Are you sure. 'They' don't look like they want you to play," she said looking at his associates who could have been the front line of the Chicago Bears.

"I'll be OK. I just have a feeling about this. I'll keep it short."

With that, he made his way through the other tables and stood next to the man at the far end. He was clearly several years older than the rest and seemed to have their attention and respect.

"Come now, play us a song! We need some levity tonight."

As he spoke, James noticed several of the others gazing around as though they were on the lookout.

"Sure," James replied, looking over to Vanessa standing with their little girl by the cafe doors. "But forgive me if my voice is a bit horse. I've been singing for a couple hours. May I sing you a song about joy?"

This clearly surprised the man, but he instantly replied, "That would be perfect. Sing to us of joy, and of praise and of love for God."

James delighted the man with a song of exactly that after which the man smiled sincerely and nearly begged him to sit down and share some tea. Feeling a bit more confident, James motioned over to Vanessa to join him.

"Now tell me about your song. Did you write it? And tell me about you and your lovely wife."

Vanessa had left their daughter in the cafe with their son and she was quite nervous about sitting with these potentially dangerous strangers. She took a seat next to James and pinched his arm as she sat. James got the message.

"Well, yes, I helped write the song along with some friends of mine. The reason I like it and like to share it is because it comes from a broken heart but not a beaten one."

"Ah-hah, I know what you mean. We must not let our difficulties overcome us. Now, please tell me your name."

"Sure. I'm James and this is Vanessa."

"Ah, how appropriate. You know Vanessa is a Greek name and means butterfly," the man smiled warmly. "My name is Abdul."

All that Abdul shared that night was that he enjoyed writing and had in fact written several books on Islam. James and Vanessa shared about why they came to Greece and that conveying the love of God was not only about words but deeds. Of course, they had no way of knowing, but that touched upon one of Abdul's 'unanswered questions' and prompted him to invite them to talk with him again in a few days. The couple agreed and over the next few months, they periodically visited with Abdul to share about what he considered the most meaningful things in life. Naturally, this led to a deep friendship, but Abdul always protected his identity. He still knew precious little about the Council and did not want to endanger his new friends.

Only a few weeks prior to their first encounter, Abdul had been approached in Brussels by a Russian man and woman who seemed to know much more about him and his 'studies' than was comfortable. They offered to provide better reasons to pursue his 'education' and to reunite him with his family. Clearly, they wanted to recruit him as they mentioned large sums of money as well.

His new assignment with the EU presidency which brought him to Athens as well as many other places in Europe and the Middle East was what made him a target, or so he thought. After several unsuccessful attempts to persuade him, they resorted to a more 'urgent' appeal:

He was sent by the EU President on a diplomatic mission to Amman for which he had been 'coached' by both Ismail and Yehuda. The morning of his departure, his 'secure' email inbox received a message which read, "Travel safely, your friends."

He didn't consider it for long as he was a bit late for the flight, but en route over the Med, the plane momentarily lost power and had to make an emergency landing in Crete. As a result, everyone on board was glad to be alive. While on the ground, another email arrived and read, "Bumpy ride?"

Abdul immediately sent a message to Yehuda along with the two emails, "Are these from you?" and explained the circumstance. A prompt reply read, "No. But I know who did. I will meet you in Amman to discuss."

Amman

Yehuda met him at the airport limo and joined him on his way to meet with FM Safadi.

"Are you familiar with the SVR, specifically Directorate S?" the Mossad agent asked.

"Of course. They do a lot of wet work and recruiting, right?" Abdul had carefully kept an eye on the SVR since he learned of their part in his government's overthrow.

"Yes, and when a recruitment goes sour, they can be very 'unfriendly'," Yehuda used the word purposely.

"Abdul, because of this, we are going to do something that's somewhat unusual for us. As you have no doubt observed, all our activities are covert by design, but in this case, we need to send a message up the chain in their organization. Typically, after they have attempted to persuade a recruit with something like this, they will re-approach. We'll be watching. Meanwhile, I'm doing some of my own recruiting - you're going to have some additional personal security from now on."

Yehuda was right. Only a day after Abdul returned to Brussels, as he was dining at "Les 4 jeudis" with a staff member, looking out the window he noticed the same two people who had first tried to recruit him, on the sidewalk approaching the corner entrance to the restaurant. Before they could reach the door, Abdul saw that the man was armed. The couple entered and surveyed the restaurant carefully, then neared the table with Abdul and his associate.

At that moment, two very large men with kitchen staff uniforms burst out and stood in front of the Russians with their backs to Abdul. At first, they gently pushed the 'recruiters' backwards with mild force. With an immediate response, the woman attacked one guard with a throat-chop and simultaneously her partner pulled his gun, firing at Abdul. The second of his new guardians knocked the arm of the assassin causing the shot to miss Abdul but wounding his associate in the shoulder. In the next few seconds, the attackers were overcome and dragged back into the kitchen. To Abdul's surprise the restaurant's maitre'd seemed unalarmed. Waiters kept serving. It was like the incident never happened. Abdul checked his associate's wound and found it to be superficial then walked him back to their office and arranged for medical treatment.

A secure text from Ismail came and read, "Everything OK now?"

"Yes, and thanks for the help. I wouldn't have expected them to raise the bar so quickly," he replied.

"They aren't accustomed to the push-back. With this, we've sent them a message that you're not available, but we'll see if they are listening. I'll stay in touch."

Athens, 30 days later

In preparing for the EU-Arab "Shared Horizons" Summit, Abdul returned to Athens. High level diplomats from the European Parliament and the Arab League depended on his coordination and facilitation. Again, the Megaron, the Athens Concert Hall in the city center served as the venue. Two days before the event, he had dined with the Greek Prime Minister who had initiated these summits along with executive representatives from the Delphi Economic Forum who were organizers.

Afterward, alone in his Hilton suite, he thought to text James and Vanessa and see if they might meet with him after the summit.

"Sure, Abdul! And may God shine light upon you and bring you joy," they replied.

He reflected upon that response and smiled. 'People so kind, in spite of their loss. While I hold on to anger and want revenge, they continually show me love and kindness,' he thought and looked forward to sharing with them.

Florence, Italy

No one really understood this man. He played the role of intercessor superbly exhibiting all the necessary false humility and kindness while underneath his heart seethed the anguish of a past that haunted him and dominated his every thought. It was fortunate for him that the Church did not truly vet its seminarians before they received the sacrament of holy orders – at least not so rigorously years ago.

The dark unfortunate truth was that his mother was raped by a Bishop and the church covered it up. She gave birth to him in an abandoned brothel on the outskirts of Rome and died in poverty when he was seven. She always told him he had a holy calling and that his true mother was the Church. But as he grew, his mind was bent on retribution. Consequently, he nursed his anger, considering it as vital to the purging from his heart anything that would get in his way.

And thus, he entered the priesthood, seeming to be an "excellent candidate", an outstanding actor with a secret goal of destroying the house of God. With so much hatred in his heart, celibacy was not a problem, though he toyed with homosexuality. What he did see was the potential for using sexual 'misconduct' to bring widespread dishonor to the clergy and so he covertly promoted it to undermine those in authority over him.

With what appeared to be an unusually rapid ascendance to the rank of Bishop and then Archbishop, he secretly encouraged sexual slavery and other abuses in the ranks of both priests and nuns, all to gain power from a network of people he controlled. For in reality, power was his god. In his mind, he imagined during the sacraments, infinite darkness indwelling him. And then, one night, it was no longer his imagination.

Under normal circumstances, his emotions were completely under control. He could laugh, cry, sing, lead mass and hear confession all in a perfect projection of empathy. However, as the evil presence approached him, his knees shook, his lips trembled, and his entire body was out of control.

That night, this unholy being found him alone in his room. As it neared, it spoke, "I hold all the power in this world, Joseph. It is mine to give and if you serve me, I will give it to you."

It was all that needed to be said. Parolin now intimately knew who he wanted to serve. At first, he was terrified but then slowly, like a consuming infection, the terror became his friend. And finally, he understood his purpose, his goal.

He realized that power over people did not reside in governments or armed forces, it did not truly come from wealth. It was supremely the result of dominating what people believed, what they worshipped and what they clung to in their hearts.

And from that moment on, he devoted himself to attaining ultimate power over the church while at the same time destroying its credibility, and in the end, to trap all the world's religions under his rule. Then when he met the Leader, he finally found the one person he could look up to.

The Leader had told him, "It's almost time."

Chapter 5

Vatican City

In his years of service in Mossad, there were few places of power Yehuda had not visited, and in many, he had carried out, albeit in the most covert manner, his assassination assignments. Sitting alone now in the Vatican library surrounded by uncountable shelves of ancient tomes, and the highly decorated multi-arched ceiling, he surprisingly felt the slightest bit intimidated. At the same time, it occurred to him that the entire city-state edifice was a grand projection of power. He mentally countered that feeling with the knowledge that he himself represented a power, though currently clandestine, that could easily rival the Vatican in scope, and refocused his mind on the task at hand.

As a result of Cardinal Tauran's recent visit with the Saudi royals in Riyadh, the Pontifical Council for Interreligious Dialogue had opened the way for the Saudi Prince to secretly recruit and nurture his own Council assets in the Vatican. Now, with the help of Dr. Ibrahim bin Abdul-Kareem Al-Issa, Secretary General of the Muslim World League, Yehuda had secured a meeting with the Vatican Secretary of State, Cardinal Joseph Parolin.

He sat rigidly on the sturdy wooden bench glancing back and forth between the black and white 'checkerboard' floor tiles and the ornate square pillar to his right upon which was painted the image of a Jewish prophet. He shook his head. Long ago, he had jettisoned what he considered the ancient defunct religion of his own people. In pondering this, he reminded himself that there was a deity he still acknowledged, but which he would never discuss.

After waiting more than an hour in the empty vacuous hall, he heard the echo of a distant door creak open and shut. Footsteps echoed as well in the huge chamber and announced the arrival of the Cardinal dressed in black robes and a large gold chain. The Secretary was clearly not in any hurry and even paused to pull a book from one of the shelves. At last, unescorted, he sat down facing Yehuda, his narrow eyes carefully examining his guest silently.

"Thank you for meeting with me, your Eminence," the greeting was perfectly presented but tasted sour in his mouth. "Is our conversation secure?" asked the Mossad agent.

"There is no audio surveillance in this chamber and the video has been stopped. No one will disturb us. Please proceed." The Cardinal shifted, indicating he found the bench as uncomfortable as Yehuda did.

"Dr. Al-Issa was quite persuasive that we should hear you out. However, I have very little time."

"Understood. My organization is aware of the long history of your attempts to build a relationship with the Russian government and the Orthodox church including your own recent visit to the Kremlin. Now, as explained by Dr. Al-Issa, we are well positioned to assist and support you in this. In fact, we believe that you will likely be the next Peter." The Cardinal stiffened and began to stand.

"Your Eminence, I realize my words are unfiltered, but they are genuine. We also believe that your efforts to reunite both 'houses' of the Universal Church will be fruitful and will make you the right choice to lead. You clearly understand the Russian mind as you recently displayed caution and tact, even making a point of visiting former Soviet states before going to the Kremlin." Parolin relaxed again and leaned forward.

"I've heard of your Council. However, it would not be wise for me to know too much, not yet. I would, though, want to be enlightened on how you would propose helping us in the reunification and why."

"In short, your Eminence, and indeed I will be brief, we have developed a significant network of assets within all fifteen Orthodox Churches who are very, let's say open to our suggestions."

Yehuda forced himself to look the Cardinal in the eye which for some strange reason was uncomfortably difficult.

"We would offer to cooperate with you in planning and possibly executing your reunification strategy and even beyond that, to accelerate your larger, much larger, interreligious ambitions. We can follow up with more detail."

"I'll consider that, but you know we will have to do the appropriate 'research' ourselves." His own stare pierced to the depth of the assassin's black heart and unnerved him. "But to the point, what do you get?"

"I'm sure your 'research' will be turn out to be compelling, and in the course of that, you will find that we, my organization, are sometimes viewed as competitive by the SVR. That makes it challenging to have a constructive dialog with them. Consequently, that's where we can help each other."

"When you come to realize how beneficial our alliance can be, we would like you to join with our friends from the Moscow Archbishop's office in arranging for us to meet with Director Naryshkin and his staff on neutral ground."

"You must have something quite important to discuss." The Cardinal got up taking one last good look at Yehuda and turned to leave. "We'll be in touch," he said, walking away. "My regards to your Leader."

Vatican City

No one came to escort him out. Yehuda sat for a few minutes and then rose to leave the way he had entered the huge library. It was still very early in the morning and the only light in the chambers was the muffled dawn hindered by the overcast sky filtering through the ancient stained-glass windows. He couldn't help feeling that despite the Cardinal's assurances, he was being watched. As he exited through the semi-secret side door, a single lamp lit as though triggered by a sensor and eerily displayed the same narrow hallway he had used to enter.

He wound his way around many turns and down several flights of stone steps. At last, wondering if he had gotten lost, he could actually feel something drawing him downward and in a direction he was sure was wrong. After a few more minutes he was convinced he was lost in the maze and thought he should return the way he'd come. The hallway was cold, very cold. Nevertheless, he ventured on, not in fear or curiosity but with a strange sense of urgency. 'This whole place gives me the creeps, and nothing gives me the creeps,' he thought.

Surely, he was under the City by this time, he guessed. Then a small room opened up having a large door. He pushed the door open and knew where he was immediately. Dimly lit and empty, he saw the tombs of the Popes. The polished marble floors reflected the lights that were directed upward, separated each by three or four meters and directed toward the low-arched ceiling. Together with the myriad ornate stone caskets, they gave a ghostly ambiance to the place. It was then that he distinctly sensed the presence that had drawn him here and it felt familiar - heavy and dark; it felt like death.

Per Ismail's instructions, he made his way to the ground level, carefully avoiding the now emerging priests and parishioners, and found the stairway to the offices of the Pope. Disguised now in robes, he spoke to no one, though as yet there were few to speak to, and avoided guards. He knew that if he was discovered, his meeting would inevitably become 'public' to the wrong agencies and that would jeopardize the entire plan. At last he saw the entrance which ultimately led to the Passetto di Borgo.

Originally built as a secret exit for the Pope back in 1277, the passageway had only been used two or three times since. The 300-meter narrow ancient stone hallway was crumbling in places which left the stone floor covered with debris, and of course, with mold and assorted dead vermin.

He exited as expected in the Castel Sant'Angelo. Removing his disguise, he found a cafe where he could get a drink and dispel the lingering sense of death. In a few moments, he texted Ismail, "Presentation accomplished. Provide backstopping to support Secretary's research. Regards to Al-Issa."

Moscow, two weeks later

Sergey was alarmed. Never one to jump to a conclusion, he nevertheless jumped on this. Why would the Vatican's Secretary of State work with his long-time friend, Patriarch Ilya III in Georgia, to arrange a meeting with the Council? Was the Vatican sympathetic to this covert sinister organization? Did Ilya realize who he was representing?

He was torn whether or not to bring this up with his boss, the President of Russia. His organization, the SVR, Russia's foreign intelligence agency, was always in a cold war of sorts with the Council and yet they knew next to nothing about its leadership or its goals. In fact, many of his agents had 'disappeared' in pursuit of more information about it.

After several days of validating the authenticity of the request, he decided to speak with the President to get a thumbs up or down. His boss didn't make him nervous; they were close friends and trusted each other implicitly. It was the issue itself that made him edgy. The CIA, Mossad, the Chinese and those inept Europeans gave him plenty of concerns. The last thing he needed was an outright war with the Council.

"Sergey, welcome. Thank you for waiting until this late hour to meet. Would you like a drink?" the President motioned to a seat in the office.

"Thank you, Mr. President. I could use one," he replied as the vodka was already pouring. "I'll get right to the point. A few days ago, I received a message from Patriarch Ilya III..."

"Yes, I know him. How is he? Still using a cane?"

"Yes, sir. Anyway, his request was for me to join him for a conference with some members of ..." he paused, "...the Council. Now, I'm sure you are aware of our frequent encounters with them in Europe, the Middle East and even in New York and Beijing."

"Sergey, I'm not going to do your job, however I know more about this Council than you probably expect. I've had contact with their Leader on a few occasions before I became President."

"Who is he? Have you met him??"

"No, not in person. He communicated with me by way of secure text and I could never trace its origin. He implied that I would one day be President and that he had many assets within our government, even in SVR."

"What?!"

"That's one reason I vetted even you so unmercifully, Sergey. When I took office, I decided we could not afford to upend the whole administration based on this man's claim but since then I'm always extra careful. I have found that this secretive Council has financial assets that rival the resources of most nation states and though they have never challenged us directly, we don't need to challenge them either. Do you know what they want?"

"No. Not yet. Apparently, Ilya is still in the dark as well. Parolin only conveyed the request to him and that it would be worth our while."

"You will go yourself?"

"Yes, sir. That's my plan. I'll bring some of my best agents... and now, based upon what you've just said, my most trusted agents."

"Good. You know, Sergey, it may be providential, we'll have to see. I've been pondering recently my desire, one we've talked about before, of extending the power of our nation southward. We must be careful and methodical of course, but we desperately need warm water ports and under the right circumstances, we could control the balance of power in energy supplies for the world."

"Yes, and you know I heartily agree."

"Thankfully, you and I are both sincere in our Orthodox faith. That's why I don't trust Rome and especially, I don't trust our Middle East partners. I'm confident we can continue to use them as we have Syria and others," the President said.

"Yes, sir. But our real confidence is in our military. We are, thanks to you, the strongest on the planet and our nuclear arsenal is unrivaled."

"Sergey, again we are of one mind. But, like I keep harping on, we must advance our technology faster. Perhaps you will be able to leverage this Council to achieve some of that?"

"I will keep it in mind, sir."

Chapter 6

Naryshkin arrived at the Orthodox Church with sheets of rain and hail pouring down. His bodyguards carefully checked the immediate area then surrounded him upon his exit from the car. Efficiently, they escorted him up the stone steps to the large center entrance of the Holy Trinity Cathedral where Patriarch Ilya III was waiting. They greeted each other ceremonially with Naryshkin deferring to the seniority of the Archbishop. Then he took another quick look around. Tblisi was much safer now than in years past but his bodyguards were as tense as if the Rose Revolution was ongoing.

"I'm so glad you could make time to meet, Sergey," Ilya welcomed the Russian SVR Director.

"We are always glad to cooperate with you, your Eminence," he replied. "This is, however, somewhat unusual."

"Let's get to my office and enjoy some hot tea."

The elderly prelate wore black robes and a tall black hat with a large red cross on its front. Using his gold headed staff, he walked slowly to the rear of the cathedral to an office with an impressive collection of gilded antiquities and two intricately carved ivory armchairs. Ilya sat in the one that appeared very much like a throne, arching almost half a meter above his head.

After tea was served and the room secured for the two men, Naryshkin stopped looking for surveillance devices and focused on his host.

"This is not Moscow, Sergey," the old man jested and smiled slightly. "No bugs."

"I'm sorry, your Eminence, it's just instinct."

"OK, so how is your family, Bogdana and young Ilya?"

"Doing very well your Eminence, and of course they would love to see you again when you visit Moscow."

"Alas, that may not happen, as I travel much less these days, but do convey my appreciation and blessing. And so, let us begin. I have urged you to listen to my guests who should be here in about an hour as I have been assured that they speak with credibility and have information to offer that we may find quite valuable."

"Valuable to both of us?"

"Well, Sergey, I'm inclined to think that it will be of more importance to you..."

"Pardon me," Naryshkin interrupted, "but tell me more about these people. You said that they were endorsed by Cardinal Parolin. Is this more a matter for the church?"

"Sergey. We've known each other for much of your life. I don't have answers to all your questions, but I do appreciate your trust. Although I chose this location, you have my permission to make the meeting as secure as you wish. The Roman," speaking of the Cardinal, "assured me that they are thoroughly vetted and that you in particular will find meeting with them worth your time. Apparently, they represent an organization much more powerful and influential than anything we've ever encountered."

Naryshkin was no longer considering this as just a favor to an old friend. He now wondered why the Council had involved the Church. The SVR knew a considerable amount about them or so he thought. Their origins were as yet unclear but for more than 40 years, they had been influencing, buying, converting, and planting assets world-wide with an almost supernatural growth. All of it was shadowed in stealth, and accomplished much more effectively than the KGB, CIA, Mossad or any other clandestine agency past or present. Just how much power they actually held was unknown, but he was confident that they had assets in every major agency and world government. Did they control nuclear weapons? How were they financed? What were there goals? Now he was glad he came.

Tblisi, later that day

'A lot of good that does now,' Sergey mused, thinking of his Tsarist ancestors. Naryshkin was intelligent with an IQ of 180 and educated in governmental, military and more recently in intelligence affairs. He was thoroughly loyal to his country; Marxism, capitalism - of course he had his preference but more than anything, his homeland itself was his lifeblood. That, he believed, was he strength. Some people didn't understand that and accused him of playing to whoever would 'butter his bread'.

Nevertheless, his loyalty to his boss, the President, and to his nation earned him high esteem in Moscow and throughout the Federation. In fact, it was one of the reasons he was so completely prepared to lead. Assignments in the military, the state and the SVR all were designed by people he'd never met and never knew to make him a potential new 'Tsar' or at least a good facsimile. His good looks, athleticism and tall stature didn't hurt either.

And rarely was he in the spotlight. He eschewed it. That's because the puppeteers in Russia, the wealthiest and most powerful all got that way through crime. He wanted power but power to control and advance his country's destiny and not simply to dance to the tune of the oligarchs' balalaika. In his position, he couldn't really stay 'below the radar' but he could avoid unwanted publicity.

What he didn't know or refused to acknowledge was that the elite had already made their decision. He was indeed destined to lead the New Russian Republic. And what he would ultimately realize was that his strength was also his weakness.

Tblisi

Just across the river via the Nikolas Baratashvili Bridge, both Israeli Councilmembers met along with Afshin at the old Ritz-Carlton, now Marriott. All three knew the city and were well aware of its strategic importance to Russia. The nearby U3 highway provided the only viable route for mechanized armaments through the formidable Greater Caucasus Mountain range separating Georgia from her northern neighbor and running all the way between the Caspian and Black Seas.

Baruch trusted Afshin more than Yehuda. He understood how he thought, his motives and ambitions. They were not dissimilar from his own - a Jew and an Iranian, both without their religious 'boat anchors' or so they thought and both with enormous aspirations. Yehuda, though a fellow Jew was not predictable and with the right motivation, would kill anyone, anyone, and enjoy it.

"Let's review," Baruch began, eyeing Yehuda who nodded. "Security at the Cathedral will be tight, but it's put together at the last minute. Our backups have been set in place including those in the Prelate's offices. Their activation code is..." he handed each of the other two a small piece of paper.

"Don't use it in any conversation unless you absolutely intend to; we don't want all hell to break loose unless we are seriously threatened. Agreed?"

"How much does Naryshkin know about us? And is he as influential as Ismail thinks with the President?" inquired Afshin.

"He knows as much as we've leaked, enough to bait our hook. And yes, he will be an effective messenger for us," answered Yehuda.

As the master strategist, this was Baruch's operation, approved by the Council and even the Leader.

"Actually, we'll offer one hook and one advisory warning, right? First, Afshin, you and I will discuss the incentives for Dreamworks. Then Yehuda will share the back-off/hands-off advice on Mahgoub. We all know Abdul has proven to be an even more effective asset than any of us anticipated. We do not want to see our 'investment' sour."

Dreamworks was Baruch's master plan to pull together an enormous and overwhelming military coalition in Syria. Mostly on schedule, his remarkable plans to plant, grow and then destroy ISIS had already worked and created the necessary power vacuum. He had also orchestrated most of the cooperation agreements between Russia, Iran and Syria, leaving the Russians a bit surprised by the course of events but convinced it was of their own doing.

"Baruch, having studied your current plan, I must confess you continue to surprise and impress me." Afshin stroked his beard and slightly shook his head.

"One day, Israel's resistance will be remembered as simply a bump in the road, my friend," Baruch replied.

Yehuda was quiet but smiled. No one ever really knew what he was thinking, only that he was more committed to the Council than anyone and had proven it many times over.

"OK, let's go," he finally offered.

Tblisi

The Archbishop's assistant shut the large door securely after which Sergey's Deputy inspected the lock and did another visual sweep of the room. All the parties were present. None of these men were unaccustomed to meetings such as this, but everyone was tense, sensing an 'ambiance' or rather a tension that 'felt' foreboding. After an uncomfortable pause of silence, Ilya spoke.

"Certainly, this is a unique meeting. Director Naryshkin and I welcome you gentlemen and look forward to a constructive and might I add informative discussion. Sergey?"

"Yes, thank you, your Eminence. General," he nodded to Baruch, "Colonel Cohen, and Ashfin, my friend." The Director smiled at the large Iranian General whom he had met several times previously. "I will of course maintain your surprising relationship with one another in the strictest confidence."

He glanced at his Deputy who stood to his left and behind him, "Understood?"

"Yes, Sir," was the prompt reply.

"Ashfin I have known for some time and seeing him here is... interesting. However, General, Colonel, I know you both only by reputation. Consequently, I would expect that you have 'backups' in place as have I."

"Director, with respect, each of us has of necessity taken the reasonable precautions, however, we are here in good faith to discuss an opportunity we are confident you, that is your country, has prepared for, but for which, we and others are also prepared... to support," Baruch replied.

This caught the Russian by surprise, and he shifted in his seat as did the Archbishop. Naryshkin had expected a challenge even a confrontation by the Israelis, not an overt offer of support. Now, he was interested. He looked at the Iranian who nodded but remained serious.

"In order to provide this support, which will be material and significant, we will want something from you. Bear with us for a moment and we'll explain our proposal fully."

It was clear that Baruch still held Naryshkin's attention.

"In the near future, a treaty draft will be presented to the Arab League, the EU President and Parliament, to the balance of the Quartet as well as to Israel and the Palestinians. Now, although this treaty will be presented by the US and Saudi Arabia, in reality, it has been developed by our organization through covert negotiations, and our assets world-wide are prepared to promote it strongly. It is, of course, comprehensive in nature, with guarantees and oversight provided by the UN, the EU, you and the US, that is, the Quartet. Financial guarantees will be provided as well as security and full diplomatic relations with both states. No more unilateral or bilateral approaches; this will be universal."

"And Iran?" the Director turned again to Ashfin.

"Bluster and posturing," offered the General, "but the real reaction will take place later."

"Our control of the media will insure that as a result of the treaty's adoption, the entire Middle East will settle. Our operatives in Afghanistan, Iraq, Egypt, Gaza, Lebanon and even Iran will ensure that nearly all threats to Israel will be quieted. As a result, the Jews will be 'lulled' into a sense of security such as they," Naryshkin noted Baruch did not say 'we', "have never known."

Yehuda added, "And as the treaty includes a mutual stand-down and partial disarmament of Arabs and Israelis, including nuclear weapons…"

"That is when we will strike," stated the Iranian General with stone-faced determination. He was obviously jubilant though. "We will amass an overwhelming force guided by your leadership. And we will coordinate and execute all the logistics so that this force will surround and pillage the Hebrews quickly - they will have no time to prepare a response."

Sergey was unsure and asked, "But what about the US?"

"The leadership of our organization," answered Baruch, "has made all the necessary preparations to effectively neutralize them and keep them from being involved. This whole campaign will finally give you dominating influence in the Middle East, access to all Israeli technology and wealth as well as friendly, warm-water ports, not to mention hegemony over the world's energy supplies."

At this, Naryshkin sunk back in the ornate chair wondering if his President's office was bugged. "We may have, indeed, done some preparation for this ourselves, but the US involvement has always deterred our operational planning." He stared at the ceiling as though lost in thought and gently waved his hand. "Media. You mentioned your control of the media. Tell me more..."

Trust me, Director, we are more thoroughly integrated even in Russia into every communication medium than any other organization in history," offered Yehuda. "And though we will certainly need much more discussion with you on the details and operational strategy of this proposal, your question offers a convenient segway into our second point." Yehuda took a sip of sweet coffee. "One of our assets has been on your radar, Abdul Mahgoub."

"Deputy to the EU President?"

"The same. He is vital to the execution of this proposal and others. Pardon me if I am forward here, but your people must back off. This is non-negotiable."

At this, Naryshkin became agitated, highly agitated.

Chapter 7

Athens

'So much life, so much joy, could heaven itself be in this little girl?' Abdul held three-year-old "Tasha" on his lap and laughed with her as she reached into his coat pocket for candy. A week after the Arab League/EU Parliament conference, Abdul's schedule was getting even more packed with new and follow up assignments including negotiations in most Mid-East capitals and then the latest, a first in-person meeting with the Council.

With a busy agenda in front of him, he wanted to see James and Vanessa who had become very dear to him. Every time he saw their little girl, he had a treat ready, and as she had come to expect it, she would run and jump into his lap, hug his neck and put out her little hand. Abdul always laughed.

Each meeting was filled with fellowship and 'philosophy'. He found his friends both sincere and thought provoking. Their discussions ranged from the essence of friendship to the convictions of faith and of course, the best of Arabic cuisine.

At first, Abdul thought it right to impress them with the beauty of Islam and its teachings and they listened to him read his poetry and prose. After this, James shared about how they had dealt with their grief through Christian faith and hope. He was always encouraging to Abdul as was Vanessa.

Eventually, Abdul wanted to simply know more about why they always made the effort to show him kindness and love. But more than anything, he was warmed by the joy that overflowed from little Tasha.

In effect, these times of friendship were like welcome oases of relief amid the growing intrigue, violence and sense of darkness he experienced as he began to get a grasp of the world-wide influence and hints of as yet unspoken plans of the Council's masters.

He had worked closely with so many government leaders and media executives to basically propagandize both Western and Middle Eastern cultures on a wide range of initiatives. With a true gift of persuasion, he could now effectively convince large numbers of people of what was true, just, kind or simply the reverse based upon the Council's direction and goals. Though he frequently reminded himself that it was all for the greater good, he struggled silently with the messaging he knew was not really true or was twisted. Some of what James had shared also gave him pause and some rang true in his heart. His friend listened but, as persuasive as Abdul was to everyone else, he never wavered in his faith. James was on such solid ground and Abdul secretly longed for that.

His 'mission' had always seemed to be for a noble cause. Fundamentally, spreading the truth of Islam was his goal or so he thought. That began to change though as he undertook assignments in negotiations and propaganda that more transparently revealed the Council's naked desire for power.

In his own deep longing to please God, some of his 'questions' still remained, and as his exposure to the methods and message of the secret organization increased, so did his discomfort. He was beginning to think James and Vanessa could help him with those questions, but he was not quite ready to be so honest.

Two weeks after the conference, he was on a plane to Tripoli. Two of his most trusted bodyguards came with him.

Tripoli

"People's Palace, driver." Abdul used the old name for the Museum of Libya. The Council's meetings were frequently in Tripoli but never in the same place. 'They must be getting more sure of themselves, meeting across the street from the Russian embassy,' he thought.

As they rode down Tariq Al Seka past the PM offices, Abdul recalled his own visits years ago as the PM of the Sudan. His day-dream was abruptly broken by a bullet smashing through the passenger-side window killing one of his bodyguards instantly. Another shot hit the car as the driver raced in a serpentine route and jerked the vehicle hard right to avoid the sniper shots. Abdul did not see where the shots were coming from but turning around, noticed another sedan chasing after them. His other guard pulled a gun out and began shooting at the pursuing car while the driver now shouted orders for assistance to someone on his radio. Another shot broke the rear window raining shards of plasticized glass inside. Abdul grabbed for the dead guard's gun and hoped his old marksmanship training would kick in.

As they passed the French embassy, they took a hard left and immediately two motorcycles appeared alongside the attackers' car and fired into it from both sides. They continued on as the vehicle of assailants crashed into a parked car and accompanied Abdul's limo the rest of the way.

Before exiting, he called Ismail.

"I've just been attacked by unknown..."

"Abdul, my men have already reported in. Rogue SVR agents who were not happy with our Tiblisi discussions."

"Tiblisi?"

"I'll explain when you arrive."

"I've just gotten to the venue. Do you still want me to come in?" Abdul asked.

"The threat is neutralized, and I've spoken with Naryshkin, rather texted him. He has begun dealing with it on his end and assures me we will not have any further incidents. Come in. We're looking forward to seeing you. Are you shaken?"

"A bit. Amani is dead."

"Too bad. He was a good asset."

Tripoli

Abdul entered the former Royal Palace, now a museum and as instructed, passed through the fog-screen display of ancient Roman statues hiding the first-floor conference room entrance. It was like walking through a hologram, or so he imagined. Inside, the room had been made secure and guards were posted outside even though the museum was closed. As he looked around, seven men, some engaged in conversation, were at the table which had two additional empty seats.

Ismail arose and pointed to the seat meant for Abdul.

"Honored Council members, thank you for making your way, once again, to our collaboration."

Abdul took his seat and just then received an urgent text from Aziz.

"My son. May Allah give you wisdom in your agreements and associations. Do not let Aliya and the children be endangered by any stubbornness."

Abdul wasn't entirely sure of what he meant and turned the phone off.

"I'm sure you all recognize our guest. His achievements and difficulties are known to many. What some of you are not aware of yet is that he has become our defacto Information Minister. His recent work includes multiple strategic treaties, important bank and media acquisitions and an all time, unexpectedly high favorability toward our message throughout Europe and even the US," Ismail boasted.

"In fact, even our associates and new partners north of the Caucasus range," everyone knew who this was, "have played with the notion of both recruiting... and retiring him. They are frankly scared by his skills, but we have reached an understanding."

"Of course, we are not scared. In fact, our dear Abdul has been the Leader's 'project' for almost twenty years now and he is pleased to see the return on our investment."

Abdul was unnerved. He took pride in what he had accomplished but was uneasy about the news of this 'investment' and what the ultimate 'return' may turn out to be. Of course, by this time, he knew of this "Leader" but here noticed the almost reverential regard that the group around him had toward this person who now appeared to be his long-time sponsor. Needless to say, he was careful to appear to everyone as the consummate statesman and pleased with the 'honors.'

Abdul spoke to the group for about thirty minutes concerning his role with the EU Presidency as Special Consultant for Middle Eastern Affairs.

After this, as he sat, Yehuda spoke, "I move to offer Council membership to Prime Minister Mahgoub." Yehuda always referred to him by his title.

"Very well," responded Ismail, "We can take a…"

"Has the Leader approved this?!" interjected Berenike who typically challenged any motion from Yehuda.

"Of course," retorted Ismail who was irritated with the Egyptian General's question. "He is, in fact, preparing for a final interview with Abdul before ratification."

"What is the basis of our understanding with the Russians?" the Saudi Prince asked solemnly.

"Our meeting in Georgia went quite well," answered Baruch, "and Naryshkin took the bait. We will wait to learn of his President's reaction. He trusts the Director implicitly or as close to that as is possible in Moscow. Part of that meeting included a 'hands-off' message concerning Mahgoub. He assured us that he will reign in his operatives."

With an 'evil eye' to Berenike, Yehuda said forcefully, "Enough of this. Once again, I move that, pending the Leader's final interview, we extend our unanimous offer to the Prime Minister."

Ismail nodded at him and looked around, "All in favor…"

All hands went up with Berenike's rising last.

Abdul hid his apprehension and smiled, thanking everyone for the unexpected honor. Later, as all parties exited, Ismail took him aside.

"Abdul, per our protocols, you have three days to formally respond to me on this offer. You mentioned that you are honored, but as yet, you do not know how small your understanding of it is. Many men have paid dearly for misunderstanding or should I say dishonoring this honor. I expect that you are smarter and more committed so there is no need to fear for yourself or your family."

Abdul tried not to show the muscles in his entire body tensing as he caught the implied threat. Nevertheless, he sensed the slightest tone of mistrust in Ismail's voice, or perhaps it was the body language.

"Meanwhile, Yehuda will keep a close eye on your security, and I will notify the Leader that we expect your positive response. After that we will arrange your face to face."

"Inshallah, I will reply very soon." Abdul said with as much confidence as he could muster.

"Yes, Yes, inshallah," Ismail muttered tersely as he left. He evidently had more important things on his mind, things Abdul didn't want to know about.

Chapter 8

Mediterranean

Blustering winds made the chopper ride extremely bumpy. When he left from Tripoli, it had been calm, but as they progressed over the Med, the weather began getting rough and the waves were large enough that Ismail doubted the helicopter could land on the yacht. In his briefcase was an encrypted drive with several things, the draft operational agreement with the Russians that the Council had worked out with the SVR, the list of senior-most Council assets with the status on their current missions, and, among other things, the nuclear launch codes for close to 500 nuclear weapons in five different countries. He also brought the software that revealed the real-time updated codes as they changed supposedly with random number generators, but in reality, by the backdoor algorithms the Council had put in place.

After forty minutes flying over the water, he was stressing out, and as they sighted the yacht, the white-capped waves were rocking the huge vessel. The pilot said loudly, "The ship's roll may be too much for a safe landing. What do you want me to do?"

"How are we on gas?" he replied just as loudly.

"Not a problem yet."

"Patch me through to the ship."

"Roger."

The pilot communicated with the ship's captain who in turn relayed the call to the man Ismail came to see.

"Ismail, we need to meet, now. Put down on the pad," came the stern, calm directive.

"You heard him," Ismail shouted to the pilot.

Suddenly, the wind abated, and the sway of the mammoth yacht stilled. In a few seconds, they were down, and as he got off the chopper, Ismail restrained his shock at the coincidental change in weather.

At 180 meters long with its own helipad and mini-sub, the Azzam, owned by Sheikh Khalifa bin Zayed cost some $600 million to build and was occasionally on loan to the Council's Leader. Ismail made his way to the plush stateroom with the help of a crew member who also verified his identity.

Upon entering, he saw the brilliantly bright room transform as the windows which surrounded it automatically darkened. As his eyes adjusted, he saw the tall man standing at the bar pouring a drink. Ismail slowly approached and accepted the offered beverage.

"Where is the drive?" the man asked calmly.

Ismail placed his case on the bar and opened the lock electronically. Retrieving a small box from it, he presented the delivery to his Leader. His heart raced.

"My Leader, the software has been thoroughly tested."

"I remind you, Ismail, do not address me like that even in private... yet. How was it tested?"

"Sir, launch codes and changes to those codes were confirmed by our assets in each of the five countries and as a further test, we launched several missiles in Iran which they thought were due to Israeli hacks."

The Leader smiled though the light was so dim, Ismail did not notice. He did notice, however, a wave of fear pass over him and a something like a hand that touched his spine. When he turned to see who it was, there was no one.

"I will review the material on the drive later. But now, tell me, how do you assess Naryshkin? Just how strong is he?"

"Our assets relayed that he followed through and pressed our proposal with the Kremlin. Initial reactions are positive but cautious."

"As predicted. Now to my first target. Are our players positioned as planned in Berlin, Paris, London and Brussels? And do they know exactly what to do?"

"Yes, sir, however we may need to adjust in Paris. The situation there continues to be unstable due to the riots. Nevertheless, we are ready to initiate on your command." Ismail was a strong fearless man and was never intimidated by anyone, anyone that is except this man – his life-long mentor. The power, supernatural power, he possessed dwarfed that projected from anyone else he'd ever encountered. Intimidation was an understatement.

Mediterranean

"The Russians will ultimately do what I want at the right time. Now, how about your conversation with Cardinal Parolin. He has a presence, does he not?"

"It's the eyes, sir. They are so dark, they're hard to read. But he came through on our request and arranged the meeting we asked for. Do you know him well, sir?"

"I know him quite well, Ismail. In fact, he has been my asset for many years. He will be an acceptable prince of my people. That's what he's been groomed to be."

Ismail swallowed almost hard enough to be heard. And at that instant, the Leader knew of his follower's apprehension.

"Our work is much bigger than you have anticipated, my friend. Be patient, you will know more in time. And speaking of time, it's time to finally place Parolin where I need him. Your next assignment is to cleanse the Vatican entirely of its wretchedness. You have one month to show me your plan to execute the Pope."

The Libyan knew what was meant by "wretchedness". For many years, they had introduced weakening elements into the church and its priesthood all over the world. The Leader wanted to purge the last vestiges of hard-line Christian beliefs and those who adhered to them. With surprising effectiveness, which he had always attributed to their patient infiltration and influence, the Council had moved the 'wretched' doctrine into the shadows and promoted a grand interfaith 'reconciliation'.

"It will be done," Ismail replied.

Following this, he updated the Leader on Yehuda's success in obtaining the tech to disable both Israel's nuclear arsenal and their defensive missile systems. It would take several months to deploy covertly but they had recruited the right assets within Mossad and within the IDF to make it happen. Of course, some credit went to Baruch as well.

Mossad, he relayed, was more deadly than ever but there were those inside in positions of power who were losing zeal for old loyalties. Yehuda and his team had nurtured these sentiments for many years.

"Afshin has been promoted so that with just one more assassination, which we will instigate Israel to execute, he will move into the position to be able to command not only most of the Revolutionary Guard military but also the huge number of civil reserve forces."

"Very good. Have you made all the deposits of the revenue obtained from the ISIS campaign?"

"Almost. It is such a large amount that our London group had to create a new conglomerate of banks to accommodate our need for secrecy. Access codes and secure IDs are already on the drive. Khan estimated another couple of months. In the meantime, we have masked it in Treasury Notes from most of the western nations. Whatever is needed for Dreamworks will be available."

"Tripoli is compromised," the Leader said with a slight hiss or whispering sound. "You need to move the operational control to...," he paused, appeared to meditate on something and then finished, "... Rome." Ismail had never seen a smile on this dark man before, but suddenly he appeared gleeful. "Yes! It's time. Rome."

Ismail was confused by this. He backed away as the Leader's wild look frightened him. As he did so, somebody grabbed his shoulders from behind and prevented his retreat. In shock, he twisted his neck - again, no one to be seen!

"And I want to see Mahgoub. It is his time as well."

Mediterranean

The room Ismail was given for a brief time to repose and "pray" was beyond all definition of plush. He did not pray, however, nor did the Leader. At least, there was no Islamic prayer by either man. Ismail was in a controlled state of panic. He had known with the Leader his whole life, but never experienced anything like this. He could see that something was actually controlling or at least motivating the man that he couldn't see. He knew that something or someone was controlling his own actions as well and that was completely unnerving.

After two hours, they reconvened at the pool. With the Sea surrounding them now calm and sunny, the Leader emerged and toweled off. He motioned for Ismail to take a seat where the stewards had placed some tea.

"The most important thing we have to cover is on the horizon, the near horizon. Within the year, I will take over the Presidency of the EU." The Leader's demeanor was once again, forceful and without emotion. "There are three who must be 'humbled' in the process. Afterwards, I will enforce a unity upon them they never imagined, and then I will turn NATO, a new 'NATO', into a force unrivaled." With this last statement, he grinned once again. Sipping his tea, he never looked at Ismail.

The rest of their time together was filled almost entirely with Ismail receiving and recording instructions on this undertaking. Not surprisingly, Abdul was going to be a fundamental part of the operation. The Leader detailed his plans for taking the 'Big Three' down, emergency elections, some of the necessary propaganda, thirteen high-level assassinations, mobilization of the migrant assets as well as both nationalist and populist leader-agents. Ismail was aghast. He typed on his keyboard furiously while his mind was overwhelmed with the genius of the complex plans.

For the first time, he began to glimpse the bigger picture, how all their programs over the last generation were coming together and nearing fulfillment. As he departed in the chopper, his terror turned to excitement with anticipation of his Leader's new world and his part in it.

Chapter 9

Athens

Abdul had no idea what the future held, only that he desperately longed for Aliya and the children. In addition, he still grieved the brutal murder of his younger brother. Alone in his suite, he spent several minutes, yet again, staring at their worn pictures in his wallet. If he hadn't been so adamant about forcing his way into political office..., he mused. But then there was the revelation of all the background activities of the Council in his life that Ismail had shared - was that all true? Perhaps it wasn't just his own passion that had guided his way. Was he nothing more than a puppet, a pawn? Ismail seemed to boast of him, then bait him, then break him over and over and it left him without anything solid to stand on so to speak. Was that part of the Council's plan too?

He looked out the large terrace windows over the cityscape that was just coming to life with the dawn. The night had been filled with restlessness and disturbing dreams. Shaking that off, he dressed for his morning meeting. On most occasions, he never spent much time studying in the mirror how he appeared, but this morning he looked disturbingly haggard. The new suit and silk tie didn't help - it was his countenance. He tried practicing a sincere smile. 'No, no good,' he thought. 'It's the eyes.'

Over the course of the last two years, he had tirelessly worked to subtly promote Islamic tenets to the western world. Combined with the decades long marginalizing of Christianity carried out by the Council-funded and now virtually controlled media, he had made headway. Recent polls showed nearly seventy percent of Europeans were now atheists. This was the first step - create the spiritual vacuum and then fill it with sympathy toward Muslim values and ultimately persuade them to adopt the new belief. 'Better, perhaps, than forced conversions...' he pondered.

Logically, it was what he always thought was pleasing to Allah. Nevertheless, as his 'Council-directed research' proceeded, he met with an increasing sense of failure in his task. He couldn't help feeling like his message was missing something, and that what was emerging all across the continent, in fact, much of the world, was an unsettling darkness in people. Mosques were being built, churches were disappearing. Wasn't that good? Suddenly, and strikingly, he was not at all sure."

"I cannot think like that," he said aloud.

Straightening his tie one more time, he left his suite and said to the guards, "We're getting breakfast."

Abdul was an early riser, but Athens is not. The city streets were empty save for the few who were hosing down and sweeping the sidewalk in front of their store or cafe. Abdul and his company made their way to the Grand Bretagne and took the elevator to the roof garden overlooking the Acropolis and Syntagma Square.

The guards ate separately but nearby. Abdul sipped his sweet coffee and began to pencil out his questions for Bartholomew I, the Ecumenical Patriarch of the nearly 300 million Orthodox Christians. As protector of Orthodoxy in the Church, he was another valuable source of information that Abdul would combine with others to craft convincing disinformation. Of course, it was all being done under the guise of ecumenical and inter-religious harmony.

His notes from more than a hundred such meetings now filled a massive hard drive. With each one, he tweaked his strategic communication plan for what Ismail called the Universal Congregation and further developed the Council's media campaign. Yehuda had called it brilliant and obviously effective, as had Ismail.

Although he'd been gone for several weeks, Athens felt more like home than anywhere outside Khartoum and he was sure he knew why. Closing his laptop, he took out his phone and dialed a familiar number.

"Hello"

"Vanessa?"

"Abdul? Is that you? It's so good to hear your voice. You know, James is out helping some people we met recently but I'm sure he'll be thrilled that you called."

"Thank you, my dear. Do you know when he might return?"

"Not for sure, but probably before noon."

"OK, that's actually just right. Do you think we all could meet for lunch? I need to speak with you."

"I think so. Abdul, are you alright?" she inquired noting some hesitancy in his voice.

"Oh, yes, yes. Just want to catch up," he quickly replied. He knew however, that he'd just lied.

"At the cafe?" she asked.

"No, not this time. I think it would be better for me to order in and we can dine in my suite."

Athens

A knock on the door announced Room Service after which two large carts of well-displayed food rolled in. About ten minutes later there was another knock clearly from the security guard outside and the door opened. Delighted to see his dear friends, Abdul hurried to greet them. Vanessa gave him a kiss on both cheeks, but then as he saw James, he exclaimed, "What happened, my friend?!"

James' left arm was in a sling and a knife wound on his neck was sown shut and bandaged but still dampened the gauze with blood. He smiled and shook Abdul's hand.

"Music critics."

"What? What do you mean?" Abdul asked.

"You remember where we first met?"

"Of course."

"Well, much like I did for you, I sang a song two nights ago and when I mentioned loving God, a man at a nearby table pulled a knife and attacked us," James relayed.

"He stabbed James," Vanessa interjected, "but before he could do more, the men James was singing for reacted and took him down. That's where he was this morning – at their home, thanking them and helping them to harvest olives."

"Harvesting?!" Abdul asked.

"Well, one-handed and..." James started to reply.

"I told him not to go. The ER doctors said his carotid artery could have easily been severed. Tell him to rest, Abdul," Vanessa complained.

"I'm fine. Really. I didn't lose much blood and the arm is just sprained."

Abdul shook his head. "And you came to see me?"

"Yes, Abdul. You see, I had a vivid dream last night about you, and then when Vanessa got your call, we both thought it was not coincidental."

They all sat down, and Abdul poured the tea.

"You know, Abdul," James continued, "we are not bashful about our following God's Son. I've shared with you how he changed my life, but it's really a process - I myself am not all that spiritual a person. I think it's maybe only two other times in my life He has spoken to me in a way that I knew was supernatural. But I'm convinced that last night was definitely from Him...," he paused, "for you."

Abdul was very solemn. Over the course of the last couple of years, they had had very honest and open discussions on the merits of Islam and Christianity. Abdul knew what they believed, but neither James or Vanessa had pushed him in any particular direction. He deeply respected that, because he could see for himself, in their lives, their love for the Almighty and for people, love which he had written and spoken much about but which, in all honesty, he did not personally know. To him, Allah was ultimately righteous and like Aziz's stern, skeptical eyes, he considered Allah watching him in the same way. Was he right? It was one of his unanswered questions.

Now, he recognized Jesus as a great prophet, but he could not accept the concept of God's Son.

"Well, you've certainly got my interest. Tell me more."

"Alright, so in my dream, there was this platform with a podium on it and you were on it reading from something and speaking, not to me, but to a lot of people I couldn't see. Then in the background was a violent thunderstorm that startled everyone, even you, and then it seemed like I was rising from the ground and looking down on you. As I arose, lightning flashed, and I saw the ground underneath you split in two and separate further and further between your legs so that you had to choose which side to stand on. Then you saw a hand, just a hand, reaching to you from the right side of the widening crevasse. You grabbed it, and as you did, a bridge formed under you. Then suddenly your family followed you on to this bridge and you all crossed over to the hand."

Abdul listened closely. He was not a superstitious person but had met more than one colleague who swore that a dream had made an impact on his life. He had never shared with his James or Vanessa what his work was about or who his associates were. All they knew was that he was an author and poet. He recognized the podium, the speaking part as referring to his Council mission and had the feeling that the crevasse beneath him was pointing to a coming decision of some sort. That part made him shiver slightly though he hid it.

"I wish I knew what it all meant, Abdul, but I don't. Perhaps you will someday," James finished.

"My friend, once again you have been very kind to share this with me. Many people would not care to do so. I will ponder it for quite some time and perhaps someday I will be able to tell you what it means."

He poured some more tea, and just then the suite's door opened again and in ran little Tasha and Michael who had been brought by Vanessa's friend. Tasha jumped into Abdul's lap as usual and stuck out her hand. He laughed and looked deeply in her bright eyes and suddenly began to tear up. A bit embarrassed, he wiped the tears away and reached in his pocket for the anticipated candy which he placed gently in her hands as well as Michael's.

She shouted, "Mommy, Daddy, Abbu gave me candy! Can I keep it?" Michael's mouth was already full.

"Of course, but now say thank you," Vanessa replied.

She giggled and gave Abdul an energetic hug. Afterwards, she went to her mother.

"You know, I... I see something so radiant in her eyes. It gives her a beauty I could never describe," Abdul said as he let her down. "It makes me think about what you said once about children and God's kingdom. Do you think Allah sees us as children?"

They all shared their ideas on many things with each other for the next few hours and then, after hugs and kisses, departed.

Athens

Upon their departure, Abdul took out his phone and sent a secure text to Ibrahim to forward to his family.

"Aliya, my heart feels empty apart from you and the children. I hope all is well. I am still safe and trusting Allah to reunite us soon. Has your father recovered completely? I just had another encouraging and thought-provoking time with my friends here in Athens. Do you have all that you need? I love you all so very much. A"

After he sent it, he felt a bit apprehensive about mentioning his friends. He shook his head and remembered he had earlier sent a message saying that he was looking forward to seeing them. Then a thought startled him, 'What if the attack on James was not just an unfortunate incident? Could the Council be keeping that close an eye on him? And could they have actually been behind it?!'

Then he also recalled informing his bodyguards of the meeting and wondered if the timing of the attack would fit such a scenario. "No, I don't think so. That better not be the case," he whispered to himself. Nevertheless, he began to watch more closely the guards and their frequent calls which he had previously presumed to be about his safety. He wasn't so sure any longer that they were around just for his protection. After all, they worked for Yehuda and he was an assassin.

He sat on the bed and prayed that Allah would protect his friends and wondered if Allah heard and if that was even an acceptable prayer. And as he prayed, he admitted to himself - he was becoming more conflicted with the righteousness of his Council directed work. He knew, nevertheless, he could never let that conflict show or impede his efforts.

Remote Sudan, nearly two years ago

At least Faheema and Amani were with her. Aliya was thankful for that, but she was determined to find a way out of the miserable compound. At first, her father had been taken with them but only a few days later, he disappeared without a word. She had no idea whether he was alive or dead.

The guards were very rough with her and the children. They beat her frequently with sticks and the children were thrown across the room when they tried to defend her. Amani was knocked unconscious once and she feared his neck may have been broken.

They were given stale oatmeal and dirty water, but Aliya strained the mud and insects from the water through her dress before letting the children drink.

About a week after they were taken something changed. The guards that first held them were shot and then new ones appeared. There were no more beatings and they began to get cleaner water, but they were still captives.

"Mama, where is Baba?? Why doesn't he come to help us?" Faheema cried.

"I don't know, my child. But you can trust that when he knows where we are, he will come and save us."

"And where did Jiddo go?" asked Amani. He loved his Grandpa. "I saw some men use a gun to force him into a truck. Will he be okay?"

Aliya just looked at him with tears in her eyes and nodded.

The new guards allowed them to walk around the compound, but they could not approach the front gate. As far as she could tell, they were the only prisoners. The former guards had had no accent, but these new ones spoke like Egyptians. That was odd because she guessed by the countryside she could see through the gate that they were in Sudan, probably in the south.

Night after lonely night, she dreamed of Abdul walking in through the front gate. He would take her in his arms and hug her and the children tightly. She loved him so dearly, and desperately she held on to the hope that he was still alive somewhere. His eyes were always so tender, and she adored his ability to create such moving poetry – he had always been an artist at heart. He was so strong and tall, and she always felt safe when he was near.

And she blamed herself for this predicament. She was the one who had pushed him into politics. Of course, it was her father's wish as well. Strange, she thought, for Aziz had never had an interest in government or policy making until one day, early in their marriage he had approach them both with almost a demand, at least a huge sense of urgency, that Abul join the party. He was so sure Abdul would be very important one day.

But she was the one who had urged him day by day, to stay the course. She believed in him. Now, she wished she had acted differently.

Then one wonderful day, some six months or more later, one of the guards presented her with a message. It was hand written, though not by Abdul, but apparently sent by him.

"Oh, my beautiful wife and dear children, I am alive and well but a long way from home. Aziz advised me to leave our country for your safety. Each day, I pray for you continually. And each night, I dream of you in my arms. I will come to you when I can, don't lose hope. Please pray for me. Your adoring husband and father. Abdul"

She clutched it and danced around the room then she read it to the children, and they danced with her. Hope was renewed. Now she knew she had to get them all out of this place somehow. She would wait no longer. She would find her husband where ever he was.

Her chance came one evening when she noticed that the guards loading crates into the back of a covered-bed truck left the tailgate down. Immediately and almost as if by instinct, she grabbed the two children and lifted them into the truck and then scrambled in herself. Covering themselves over with burlap, they hid until they heard the tailgate close and the truck began to move.

Peering out the back, she noticed a road sign indicating El Gadarif was nearby. She knew then that they were at least several hundred kilometers from Khartoum. As the truck came to a halt, they all climbed out and ran into the town even as dusk fell.

It was August and hot though not as hot as Khartoum. The overcast sky threatened rain and all around the countryside was semi-arid bordering on desert. Grasses and scrub acacia trees and bushes were interspersed with cultivated fields. The outskirts of town consisted mostly of the typical thatched roof huts of farmers scratching out a living on cotton.

The only way to find food and shelter was through the kindness of the people who barely had enough to feed their families. Aliya kept a close eye on the children knowing they would be hunted by their captors as well as the occasional leopard or lion. They saw a variety of antelope and guinea fowl along the way and knew they must be close to the Dinder National Park and the Dinder river.

She tried not to show the children any fear, but she was indeed fearful. She had no idea what to do or where to go. After hours of walking, dusk was approaching, and she knew they had to find shelter. Finally, as she approached a small group of huts, she noticed people still milling about and suddenly an old farmer passed her coming from the fields behind.

"Umi, where are you going?" he said, addressing her as a young mother.

"Oh Hajj, we are lost and running from some very bad men."

Without a moment's hesitation, he answered, "You must come with me. Under my roof, you will be safe. Come, come!"

"You are so kind. Thank you so much," she said with tears on her cheeks. She ushered the children behind the white-haired man to a distant hut where his family welcomed them warmly. The next day, as she helped make a breakfast, a neighbor entered the hut and looked at her with a hint of recognition.

"You look so familiar," she said as she gazed at the children as well. "My husband's brother took us to the capital last year and we saw you and your husband at a rally by the Umma Party. Am I right?"

"I can't say for sure. Who do think we are?"

"You look very much like the Prime Minister's wife, but you are so skinny now, perhaps I am mistaken."

Aliya didn't know whether or not to be forthright. Could this woman have any relations with their captors? Just as she was pondering how to answer, the old man came into the hut with a bowl of rice. He quickly assessed the situation and sagely intervened.

"My home, my guest, Aarifa. Don't dishonor us with these questions."

The woman, perturbed, silently excused herself and left. The man gently touched Aliya on the forearm and said, "She is harmless. No one would believe her anyway. If you want to tell me anything, you may. I am poor but I love this country just like your husband," he said quietly and smiled. "Now, how can I help?"

"We were being held as prisoners in a compound several kilometers to the north. I don't know who was in charge or who to trust and I fear the worst for my husband. Do you know anything about him?"

"Oh, no, no, my dear. Out here, we rarely get much news of the events in Khartoum. But I can ask around, quietly of course. I will make sure you and your children are safe here."

Aliya began to weep. All the stress that had built up for weeks and longer erupted. The old man called his wife and they sat Aliya down on a pillow. The wife mildly scolded the old man, thinking he had caused the outburst, but Aliya spoke up, "No, no, it's not his fault. You both are just so kind. I shouldn't cry but I'm honestly so afraid for Abdul and my father. We can't go back to Khartoum. Not now. But where are we to go??"

"Hasim, we must help her," the wife insisted.

"Yes, of course. As I just told her, first I will try to find out what I can about her husband. Meanwhile you can send for Abdullah."

"Abdullah?? Are you sure?"

"Yes. You know he is a good man. Now go on."

The wife showed Aliya where food and drink could be found for the children and then left the hut. As she reached the old dirt road, she waved down a truck and got in. After she departed, Aliya felt a little less alone but worried she was endangering this humble couple.

That night, the old man, Asim, relayed that he had found out from people who worked at the compound that the "old man" briefly under guard there was now dead. Aliya knew that it must have been her father. He also learned that Abdul had left for Egypt but where exactly or for what purpose he couldn't tell.

Two days later, in the late morning, she noticed another truck turn off the road into the village. The elder couple were out working in the fields and the garden. Two armed men got out and walked to the nearest hut. Aliya shuddered and ran to retrieve the children who were outside and to the rear of the hut for she recognized the men as guards from the compound. She and the kids hid in another hut and watched as someone directed the two guards toward her hosts' dwelling. They took out their pistols as they approached and entered the hut.

Aliya's heart raced as she watched and firmly stilled questions from the children. Soon, the men reemerged, looked around the village, reholstered their guns and headed back to their truck. Before they left, it seemed like they looked around again as if they expected to see her hiding.

That evening, the old man welcomed his friend Abdullah and introduced him to Aliyah. His eyes opened wide when he recognized her.

"Asim, do you realize how much danger you are in with Madam Mahgoub here?"

He was apparently from the South, a handsome man with modestly graying hair and a strangely joyous face. In spite of his question, he reflected kindness and a calm demeanor. He spoke, however, with broken Arabic.

"Abdullah, that is why we called you to come. You have often told us of how your God is loving and helps those in need. Well, here's a need. Now, what can you do?"

Shortly, Aliyah was informed that Abdullah was a missionary from Kenya who traveled in the southern part of the country. His real name was Joseph, but he used Abdullah while in Sudan.

"I have friends near the border who will care for her. She'll be safer there. Madam…"

"Please call me Aliya."

"OK, Aliya, can you get your children and anything you came with? We should be off immediately."

Aliya looked to her hosts who nodded and confirmed she would be in good hands with Abdullah. In fifteen minutes, they had piled into his car which had more miles on it than any she'd ever seen and were off, heading southeast. They drove all night over terribly bumpy roads and arrived at the border town at dawn.

As they arrived, there was trouble. The friends dwelling was under siege by a hostile group of men with clubs and torches. They were yelling that the infidels had to die. Aliyah could hear children screaming to their parents, but the attackers were merciless. Soon the hut was on fire and the entry was barricaded.

Abdullah ran to the scene leaving his jalopy some 200 yards away. He pushed the angry men aside and tried to get to the blocked doorway but was soon overwhelmed and beaten to death by the crowd. Aliyah watched in horror.

And then, horror of horrors, Amani had disappeared. She screamed out for him, then noticed that he was running to help Abdullah who by this time was bleeding out.

"What's he thinking??!" she cried. "Stay here, Faheema!" she exclaimed while slamming the car door shut and running after her son.

Twenty meters from the crowd, she caught up to him, but also caught the eye of the ringleader of the gang. He swung around and charged toward her.

Chapter 10

Secret bunker in Israel

"One tactical nuke even in the mountain's entrance would effectively neutralize the facility, General."

In a top-secret bunker deep below Israel's Dimona nuclear facility south of Hebron, Baruch held an emergency planning meeting sanctioned by the new hawkish Minister of Defense. The Prime Minister had gone public with extensive documentation proving the deceptive nature of Iran's advancing nuclear program and though there were some 'raised eyebrows' around the world, the media seemed largely to ignore it. Thus, the word from the top was for Baruch to plan a unilateral response.

Of course, this dovetailed perfectly into his ongoing Council directives, and as his senior staff brought forth the options, he was thinking well ahead of them.

"Are the modified F-16Is ready with conformal tanks?" he asked.

"Yes, sir. The lessons learned in Operation Wooden Leg helped us prove their longer range."

"Escorts?"

"Yes, F-35 Lightning IIs stealth fighters to be refueled en route and carrying our newest jamming tech that will confuse the S-400s and all interdiction forces."

"Pilots?"

"Sir, we've tested, screened and selected the most capable. Lt.Col. Yaakov Katz will pilot the bomber."

"I have met Katz. His reputation is impressive," Baruch replied. "Didn't he recently fly the stealth mission over Lebanon?"

"Yes, sir. He was the team leader."

Other IDF Generals were in the room as well but since this was an operational strategy meeting, Baruch was in charge and reported directly to the Minister of Defense. Back-up and contingency planning were active with ground, naval and missile forces readied. Israel had never used a nuclear weapon like this before. To play their hand would not surprise any major power as to their possession of the weapon, but it would certainly bring a thunderous world response. It would also radically change the Middle East.

'This will play out just as the Leader planned,' he mused even as his chief of staff briefed him.

"Casualties and collateral?" he asked the Colonel.

"In the Fordow facility and in Qom, approximately twelve to fifteen hundred plus another 300 or so when we take out the SPND nuclear research facility in Tehran."

"Colonel, we need to lower those numbers. The first use of a nuke in the Middle East will not go well on the world stage, let alone the optics associated with casualties in Qom and Tehran."

"Understood, General. We can also incorporate improved targeting from our new satellite."

Baruch listened for another twenty minutes, then conferred with the other commanding officers including those from Mossad. His next meeting in Tel Aviv was approaching and it would be nearly as challenging.

Tel Aviv

Baruch arrived by helicopter to HaKirya and went directly to the twelfth level underground where another meeting was due to begin. Unlike the first, this one was led by Mossad together with the IDF systems defense team. He recalled their glee after the success of the Stuxnet worm which exploited zero-day vulnerabilities of the Iranians' computer operating systems. Now, the challenge was to not only take down systems associated with their nuclear programs but to cripple the entire Iranian infrastructure from the telecommunications systems down to school room computers and to keep them inoperable. The intent was to keep Iran from being able to wage modern warfare now and well into the future.

Unknown to these people was the fact that Baruch had already briefed Asfin, so that as the new leader of Quds and Basij, he was covertly preparing on his end to make the new Israeli weapon maximally effective as well as disabling as much of the Iranian missile forces as possible. Baruch shook his head slightly at the irony and as he pondered this, was amazed at the Leader's foresight and strategies.

Baruch noted Yehuda in the room as well. Per Council protocol, he did not acknowledge him and frankly was a bit surprised as systems countermeasures were not his area of expertise. Nevertheless, as the meeting progressed, it became obvious why he was there. One of the key factors in the success of the mission was the ability to assassinate all Iranian scientists that could hinder the deployment of the virus or successfully purge it.

As a planner, Yehuda outlined his targets, twenty-six in all, that would be taken out beforehand and within minutes of the deployment. Ideally, the virus deployment operation would be executed almost immediately after the nuclear attack so that it could be disguised as a result of the bombing rather than as a separate initiative.

'I'm sure that will happen exactly as planned. He's very good,' Baruch thought.

Coding challenges that had to be overcome were presented in excruciating detail from one of the most senior data specialists, a surprisingly attractive Captain Tamar Mintz. Though Baruch was not following the detail, he was impressed with her knowledge of the material. Clearly, she was some sort of super-nerd.

Wrapping up, Baruch briefed everyone that timing was crucial to overall effectiveness and mentioned that he had received a green light to execute 'Little Samson' based upon this groups' ability to deploy the new virus in synchrony. A final go-trigger would come from the PM.

After a short conference among the systems defense people, best guess was ten to twelve weeks to finish testing and figure out all the deployment logistics. Baruch allowed himself a quick glance at Yehuda who nodded slightly and covered it with a shallow cough.

"Captain!" Tamar, along with the rest of the systems staff had just exited the facility when Baruch called her. She turned and saluted. The General returned the salute.

"Yes, General."

"I'm glad I caught you. Your presentation was impressive. I want to see you in my office to review it again. So much rides on this." She was indeed a stunningly beautiful woman, and thus his order was not entirely professionally motivated. Pondering her skills, he also wondered if she might become a future Council asset. "My aide will let you know when."

"Of course, General. I'll be ready."

Tamar recognized the look in his eye and knew she would have to be careful.

Sdot Ha'ela AFB

IDF Air Force Commander Maj General Yosef Eshel and Col. Benyamin spoke to the pilots who were to fly the bombing run into Iran. Lt. Col. Katz was the team leader. Together with the other 17 pilots, co-pilots and alternates, he listened attentively.

"This is not only a historic mission, gentlemen and ladies," the General began, "it is one that will alter every aspect of our lives from this day on. From military posturing and readiness to politics to superpower support and/or adversity to economics to... well the list goes on. Everything is going to change. And our nation will either survive and thrive or we will be destroyed by our enemies. Never before have we contemplated conducting such a mission with weapons so powerful. Make no mistake, this will not be a declaration of war. We are at war. We have an enemy that has vowed repeatedly to the world to annihilate us. Europe has allowed them to continue their quest to develop that capability. The PM and the entire cabinet are in agreement. We must eliminate the threat at all costs."

Col. Benyamin added, "You've all been briefed on your flight plans and refueling. We're confident you'll need to jam S-300 and 400 signals but be prepared at any time to go hyperstealth. As we have learned before, the return flight will be present some challenges. We want you ALL back in one piece. Wheels up in 15."

The group stood in unison as the General and Colonel exited.

At this point with other missions, the room would have been filled with chatter. This time, silence. It was sobriety, not fear. Yaakov was focused and intense as was every other pilot.

After a final inspection with special attention to the ordinance, he and his co-pilot Maj. Talia Dahan climbed aboard. The normally single pilot F-16 had been customized to accommodate the second 'chair' and had the benefit of the hyperstealth modification tech. IAF techs had labored all night to prepare the planes, checking, double and triple checking all systems.

As the aircraft exited the HAS, Hardened Aircraft Shelter, and lined up for take-off, everyone was operating in perfect precision. There was only a final radio confirmation from the Colonel to Yaakov and quickly they were off. One after another, pilots with their jets roared upward as if everything they held dear was at stake.

They sped northward over the Med between Cyprus and Syria, then proceeded eastward along the Turkey-Syria border. Finally, they crossed over northern Iraq and into Iran. The tankers loitered behind and were ready to refuel on the return trip. The aircraft was heavy, very heavy. Yaakov could feel it and knew stealth was his only defense until the craft lightened.

As they approached Fordow, his heart raced uncontrollably. He never imagined that he would be the one to initiate a nuclear war; shaking off the imagination, he refocused his mind.

"Major, begin target acquisition," he said firmly.

"Yes sir. As soon as the bunker buster does its work, we'll be ready," she replied.

A second aircraft, a bomber, was equipped with the heavy ordinance, recently developed by Israel's own Rafael Corporation and kept secret from the US. Equipped with new penetration tech, the enormous conventional bomb would hit the Fordow site first creating a crater which would help to focus the following nuclear blast and reduce at least slightly the spread of radioactive fallout in the region.

"Permission to engage, Colonel?" came over the radio from the bomber.

"Granted. Good hunting," he replied with as calm as voice as he could muster.

In the distance shortly afterward, they could see the enormous explosion with a cloud that appeared almost nuclear.

"Your turn, sir," the bomber's pilot radioed back.

Stealth was no good at this point as the sky lit up with antiaircraft fire. Yaakov danced his aircraft through the chaff. 'Like dancing with an elephant!' he thought.

He had to pass into the buster's cloud to lay the nuke in the best location.

"Got it!" shouted Talia.

Immediately, as if muscle memory took over, Yaakov let the nuke fly, then lifted his aircraft in a radical upward turn that nearly made both of them faint. In a moment, the satellite guided ordinance exploded perfectly. Roaring at a tremendous speed, they made it just out of the immediate blast radius, but their plane almost burst apart with the shock wave so that both pilots had to work to keep it in the air. The light was blinding, and heat dissolved or melted the entire mountain behind them. If anyone or anything survived below, they would soon perish from radiation or suffocation. Fordow was gone.

The return trip required all the aircraft, including those that bombed the SPND to return in a below-radar path out of Iran winding south of Tabriz and then soaring to 40,000 feet over eastern Turkey. They soon lowered to tanker altitude and refueled. Yaakov and Talia's plane however could not completely refuel as the nuclear blast shock wave had damaged their conformal tank's refueling port. They were able to make it back out over the Med but had to eject at a very risky speed. Fortunately, they were rescued by helicopters from the US Sixth Fleet.

Returning home, they were quietly welcomed as heroes but as predicted, the world and especially the Middle East was indeed a different place.

National Cyber Defense Authority, Israel

Though a defense agency, the NCDA was home to Major Tamar Mintz's team of malware specialists who developed offensive cyber weapons. In a highly coordinated effort, Mossad agents delivered the new Pan virus to their Iranian assets who in turn deployed it to more than 4800 computer systems in Iran's military, communications and nuclear industry sectors. The scary thing was that the virus had proven to be so persistent in test that even Tamar's team had nearly lost control and had to physically destroy their test systems. It was probably too good, for they had enabled it to replicate upon every conceivable trigger and around every known countermeasure. Like an airborne virus, it also propagated wirelessly via wi-fi, bluetooth and cellular signals.

As predicted, and in non-coincidental timing with the bombing attack, the virus froze all systems and corrupted data nationwide in Iran. Spreading like wildfire, it somehow infected even isolated systems. As a consequence, military operations, in order to respond to the bombing had to resort to stone-age communications methods and prompted Revolutionary Guard commanders at the senior levels to seek guidance on activating foreign allies, specifically Hezbollah, or to stand down and regroup. Chaos reigned.

Meanwhile Ashfin's warnings of just such a situation and his own apparently resilient command and control operations boosted his status amongst the country's leadership immensely. Secure communications with Baruch were still working much to both Generals' satisfaction.

Tehran

"Chang just arrived. His jet had to land without tower control," Ashfin's aide informed him.

Both Symantec and TrendMicro were paid enormous sums to clean the Pan virus. Chang owned the latter company. The just in time arrival made Ashfin appear nearly clairvoyant. He had pressed the IRG to bring them to enhance the military's security. Their combined efforts, however, were to no avail as Pan was unlike anything previously observed.

Unknown to Israeli Cyber Defense, Baruch had given Ashfin a system access backdoor code that could be used to immunize a limited number of systems. This he used carefully to keep his own command only partially impacted, just enough to aid his ruse of being 'ahead of the game' and in control, but not too much so as to reveal the subterfuge.

That being said, the country was a mess. Air traffic stopped, all transportation control or automation ceased. The power grid went dark. Telecommunications were at best sporadic and thus all commerce that required it came to a halt. Food was in short supply, crowds rioted for clean water and other basic necessities. The government seemed virtually neutered. Government controlled news was silent.

Ashfin, on the other hand, put his troops on alert and reinforced the security of the government offices in Tehran. He was also able to have enough communication capability to prepare a limited number of missiles for launch but unable to target them.

When the dust began to settle, he was 'miraculously' able to revive hospital systems and certain hardwired telecommunications. The image created was that he was apparently more capable in resolving the crisis than anyone else and this wasn't wasted on the government or the people. He became an overnight hero. Handwritten notes delivered by courier from his boss and the President congratulated him and soon he was granted significantly greater authority.

Central Israel

In a shielded and secure room at NCDA, Major Mintz and two of her senior team members, together with General Baruch and his aide, discussed the outcome as intelligence continued to come in. The General had two things on his mind - the operational status and the Major.

"Can we get an update from Director Cohen's team?" he asked his aide impatiently. Cohen headed Mossad and of course had the freshest intel on what was happening in-country.

"On it, sir." The Aide replied and exited the room.

The General turned to Tamar.

"Well, it would appear that congratulations may be in order, Major," he said, ignoring the other two in the room. "Now, remind me, how is the virus contained to Iran?"

"The virus is self-managing, sir, and by comparing native language documentation and specific root files, it knows whether to activate or merely propagate. It will infect every system on the planet. The code itself continually mutates to avoid detection in many file types. Thus, it will indeed go beyond the borders of Iran, but we know the mutation sequence algorithm and can stop the propagation. We learned that the hard way."

Baruch already knew all of that, but the explanation gave him the excuse to carefully 'examine' the Major which he did not disguise well. Recognizing his body language and the 'inappropriate' look, she turned her attention to Captain Rabin, her associate.

"Captain, please chime in. Can you further explain the cross-code comparatives?"

The discussion continued drilling deeper into detail Baruch mentally dismissed. After a few more minutes, his Aide returned. He whispered to the General something that quickly got his attention and with a terse excuse, he left the room.

The not so subtle come-on to Tamar left her skin crawling. She knew of Baruch's reputation for ruthlessness and 'off the book' operations. A few moments later, the Aide stuck his head in.

"You are dismissed."

Tamar and her team should have been feeling proud of their accomplishment, but the exchange left them all feeling 'uncomfortable'. They dispersed and returned to their work areas and Tamar reported back to the Cyber Ops Center where she learned Baruch had returned to the IAF Operational Command site. That news actually made her feel better, but she remembered that she was still on standby to meet with him personally. She decided not to mention that to anyone... yet. After all, the country was at war.

Instead, she quietly prayed and remembered her sister who had shared this new faith with her and the power of prayer.

Tripoli

Per the Leader's instructions, Ismail worked furiously to move the Council's office out of Libya to the new location in Rome. He had very limited help due the need to maintain extreme secrecy. Even the Council members themselves did not yet know the new site.

All over the news was the story of a nuclear attack on Iran by Israel and the crippling of the country's entire infrastructure. Sunnis in many Arab capitals celebrated while Shiites vowed revenge. Every capital around the world shuddered, anticipating escalation.

Ismail, of course, expected all this, but his nerves were still on edge. As he packed, a secure communique came in from Baruch:

"Dreamworks proceeding as planned. Bombing accurate and completely effective. Pan better than predicted. We will see it spread to our other intended targets and will have control of its activation when needed. May have a new asset. Will keep you informed."

Chapter 11

Remote Location in Italy

As he walked down the beautifully decorated hallway of the Pope's summer palace, he appreciated the ornate arched partitions with their scenic paintings, all in perfect condition. Stopping at one of the balconies, he enjoyed the view of the large lake. A moment later, Abdul's escort tapped his shoulder.

"Mi scusi, Signore. Il Cardinale - aspettando."

"Oh, of course," he replied.

Down the impressive corridor and to the left was a room, well-appointed but smaller than he expected, where Cardinal Parolin sat with two cups of sweet coffee and an impatient expression.

"Prime Minister," he began, "I'm very interested to hear your thoughts on our future cooperation, especially concerning what we are calling... the common faith."

Abdul recognized the diplomatic phrase for the One Common God ideology, and as he sat, he first took a sip of the coffee. He had learned from previous encounters that although the Vatican's Secretary of State was vague and non-committal in public, in private he was direct and wanted directness from whom ever spoke with him.

"To the point, as usual, your Eminence. As we discussed earlier, I have made a detailed analysis of the commonalities of Islamic and Christian teachings for you and identified the points that can be emphasized to persuade your listeners to accept closer cooperation with Islamic clerics, even to the point of approaching integration of the faiths. I have also specified the things that Muslims, both Sunni and Shiite, will want to hear and not hear."

Abdul's understanding of this work was that it would ultimately lead to the domination theologically of Islam over Christianity and ultimately, over all other faiths. Thus, for him, it seemed to be the best use of his talents in service to Allah. He would never have dreamed of this opportunity a few years ago. Nevertheless, working with this man somehow made him feel guilty and dirty.

The contrast between what he sensed spiritually in 'His Eminence' and the simple sincerity of James and Vanessa couldn't have been greater. Because of that, he was knotted up inside. In his mind, he justified his cooperation with the Secretary, but in his heart, he was coming to abhor it. Of course, he couldn't show his feelings, for his family's safety depended on his work and commitment to the Council.

Fundamentally, Abdul did not consider himself a deceiver. He was a master of influence and persuasion but always upon what he thought to be the truth. He had taught his children the truth, he had preached it, wrote about it. Despite that, he knew he had no relationship with God as James talked about. That was really a foreign concept that he realized many if not most westerners also disregarded, but he consoled himself in believing his truth.

It was easy to imagine why Ismail spoke of Christian beliefs as "wretched" when he considered this powerful leader of the Church. But then James and Vanessa were totally different. He wondered how Ismail would interact with them and shuddered.

"Mahgoub! Are you with me?" The Cardinal was irritated with Abdul's momentary musing.

"Your Eminence, here is the draft agenda for the Common Faith dialog with the major Islamic and Christian leaders in Jerusalem next month." Abdul recovered his focus quickly and handed the folder to the Prelate.

"Have you arranged for the facility in East Jerusalem I mentioned?" the Cardinal asked.

Meeting in the Palestinian portion of the city would clearly send the message that the Jews had nothing yet to offer in this forum, and would allow for more secrecy, at least theoretically.

"Yes, the Rockefeller Archaeological Museum is booked under Dr. Ibrahim bin Abdul-Kareem Al-Issa who is co-hosting the event with you."

"That's satisfactory." The Cardinal put his coffee down and leaned forward slightly, looking directly into Abdul's eyes. Abdul thought he recognized the look, it reminded him of Aziz. But there was more. It wasn't just a distrusting glare; it was as though the man was trying to project fear.

"Give me your hand, Prime Minister. I'll give you a blessing."

Abdul slowly offered his right hand, which Parolin turned palm up. Next, the Cardinal took an odd shaped icon with Akkadian language symbols from his robe and placed it in Abdul's hand.

"A Solar seal to protect you from the 36 decans," he said. "Now, your blessing. Melach Ba'al. Melach Ba'al. Give this man your power to deceive. Give him your wisdom," he pronounced in a whisper, then repeated it, and then looked again in Abdul's face. "An ancient blessing," he smiled. "You have indeed been very crafty in your unique position with the EU and in your relationships with the Muslim World League. Now, you will be even more effective... and useful."

Abdul was shocked and strangely, he shivered. He didn't know what to think, but held that expression back, knowing it would leave lingering questions in the Cardinal's mind. He forced a smile and nodded.

"Thank you, your Eminence."

Immediately, the Prelate stood and exited the room leaving Abdul feeling intensely anxious. Staring at the old Babylonian amulet in his hand, he noticed that it felt hot. He put it in his pocket, gathered his materials and left the palace sprightly.

As he left the superbly landscaped grounds, he stopped again to gaze upon the lavish estate. In contrast to his first impression of awe, he now saw it all as a mask hiding the decrepit nature of the person inside. Some believed deception was a legitimate means to an end. He did not.

Then it occurred to him that his father in law had discussed this with him and proposed that Abdul use any and all means to promote the faith.

It was years ago, but the consequent disagreement that ensued left an ugly scar on his memory and suddenly, his own conscience rang out that 'Aziz is watching' and that he was right all along.

Was it his conscience? Or just a hangover from his Parolin interlude? Did he believe that deception was somehow justified now? No! But hadn't he used his skills to twist the truth? No! Maybe. No.

He felt dirty and somewhat confused. What was truth and what was a lie? Was his gift to spin the truth to make it appear as a message he wanted, was that deception or only a means to greater truth? What was the nature of truth? James spoke of the truth being spoken in love, he called it "all truth".

He did not want to truly deceive, and he certainly did not want more power to do that. He fumbled in his pocket and pulled the amulet out again. It began to burn in his palm. Violently, he cast it into the foliage as far away as possible. As he did so, he became scared that someone had seen him.

But how could he accomplish the goals of the Council, the marginalizing of the 'wretched' and the acceptance of a worldwide faith, worldwide unity, without 'a spin'? Islam had many views. So did the 'wretched'. He had always believed he held to the truth but was it truth nested in or born out of love? Did the end really justify what he was doing and what the burning amulet symbolized?

He thought to pray but he also seemed to see both Aziz and Parolin watching his life and it so disgusted him, he could not. 'I must be more discerning!' he thought but there was still a struggle for he knew Aliya, Faheema and Amani were depending on him.

Khartoum

Always an angry man, Aziz was used to pushing others around and to using his anger as a means of intimidation. That had always worked for him until recently. It was when he met the Libyan that his 'style' changed. It had to. There was an intensity in the man that made Aziz shrink. It wasn't about Islam; it was a matter of power.

Ismail was his name and at first, he came off as a true believer. He frequently complimented Aziz on his spiritual status and his grasp of the Quran. Then came the 'little favors' for which he was generously rewarded. Aziz never understood how easy he was to manipulate as the man played upon his ego and desire for money.

Eventually, he was introduced to associates of Ismail who relayed requests which became more and more like instructions and then directions. When Aziz chaffed or felt the demands were demeaning, he learned quickly and with severity the consequences. And his reward for compliance – he and his loved ones were allowed to live. When he learned of Ismail's interest in Abdul, he was both fearful and jealous. And then, when he was instructed to send his son-in-law out of the country, he realized the relationship was a massive mistake. He knew however, the threats were real, and he obeyed. Later, he was taken by mistake along with Aliya and the children to the compound and then released.

Having served his purpose, he met his end while walking home after evening prayers. Sadly, despite his inflated sense of self-importance, no one really noticed or cared about his demise. Police called it a mugging and even as he lay semi-conscious next to filthy cans of restaurant garbage, he knew Ismail had ordered it and with his last thoughts, he longed to hold his grandchildren.

Southeastern Sudan

Operating on instinct and adrenaline, Aliya grabbed Amani and carried him to the truck tossing him unceremoniously inside.

"How could you do something so crazy?!"

"Mama, it's what Baba would do. I had to help that man!"

She wasn't used to driving but she started the engine and pushed hard on the gas pedal, at least she thought it was the gas pedal. The truck jumped forward and charged toward the crowd which now split in all directions fleeing in fear. The man charging her didn't make it out of the way and soon there was a 'bump-bump' as the vehicle ran over him.

Aliya was partly crying and partly yelling at the children to hold on as the truck went faster and faster on the pot-holed road. In a few minutes, the remnants of the angry crowd had been left behind and she was getting more used to how to drive. In the morning light she could see the hills in the distance and hoped that they meant they were closer to the border.

She knew they would have to abandon the vehicle and cross the border on foot. How could they cross without being recognized? Where would they go after that? Could she find shelter and food for the children? 'No, we must find Abdul! I cannot give in to fear,' she thought.

As she finally seemed to settle her heart, she looked in the rearview mirror and gasped, "Oh no!"

Another truck was approaching at high speed.

Roma

Back in his hotel suite, Abdul studied the amulet and wondered why a Christian Cardinal would use an ancient Babylonian token to pronounce his odd 'blessing'. Taking out his laptop, he wrote what he thought would be a securely encrypted email.

"My dear James and Vanessa,

My heart longs for your fellowship. There is a genuine warmth in your hearts when we share together. I must tell you, I fear that my wife is danger. I have not heard from her in three weeks now and when I do, it does not seem to be her writing. I used to get messages from my children but that has ended too. I'm very worried. My father-in-law does not reply to my inquiries either. You know that I have spent my whole life seeking to please Allah but increasingly, I am uncertain about what I'm doing. My path has become more clouded. I have written things that I was convinced were truthful and righteous but the more I consider you two, the more I think I'm missing the mark. Please pray for my family and please pray for me. I want so much to do what's right. With deepest love, Abdul"

After sending the message, it occurred to him that he had never included in any message his inner conflict. And suddenly, he was worried that his communication may have made the situation worse. Did the Council monitor these emails? Had he just done something incredibly stupid?

Chapter 12

Palmachim Airbase, Israel

Shaldag was founded in 1974 in the aftermath of the Yom Kippur War. As the unit dedicated to clandestine deployments into hostile environments, it was home base for Col. Katz. In the aftermath of the Fordow bombing, Yaacov was to some, a hero, but to others, including himself, the jury was still out.

As much as the government tried to mask his identity, both he and Talia were widely known as the ones who 'brought the hammer' to Iran. In spite of that, he felt safe, most of the time. Of course, as the smoke cleared literally and figuratively, Iran vowed to rain fire on Israel but was in no position to make good on that just yet. Transportation and communications were still down weeks afterwards. Iranian agents in Syria and Lebanon were acting independently.

The Middle East did change. It didn't blow up, yet. In fact, it was very strangely quiet, all things considered. News reports showed the expected mass demonstrations in Tehran and Gaza. The UN was in chaos. According to intelligence reports, the Russians had not made any moves; neither had NATO although both had gone to states of heighten preparedness and had warned each other to be rational. The Knesset was livid, but so what else was new? Katz was relieved to some extent. He honestly expected the regional tinderbox to explode but it did not. It almost seemed like the whole Muslim world had stepped back, aghast and intimidated.

Personal thanks came securely to Yaakov not only from the PM, but from the Saudis and the Gulf States. So much for secrecy. It was odd that General Baruch delivered the message from a Saudi prince personally.

Yaakov had not slept well since the mission. He knew the stakes were high when he was called upon and he was not in any sense weak-kneed. Not only was he an experienced pilot and wing commander, he was a martial arts expert, a superb marksman and held the highest clearance possible in the IAF. That being said, no one had ever used a nuclear weapon in the Middle East before. It was not just another bombing run and he could not clear his memory of the ferocity of the blast as well as his fear that the same thing would come back to his country.

After a week of sleeplessness, his mind wandered more easily. Oddly, he recalled his parents who were killed in a terrorist attack when he was eight. A mindless, senseless bus-bomb. He himself had been injured but being sheltered by his father, he had survived. Growing up after that in his Uncle's house, he became extremely hard and rebellious. Persistent sorrow beat upon his heart until the emotional scar-tissue became impenetrable. Fortunately, he found his relief in the military. In this pursuit, his life took on a purpose that gave him a drive to make his mark, to make a difference - a real difference.

He had no deep religious convictions, most Jews did not. Raised in Jerusalem, he witnessed the brazen commercialization of both Hebrew and Christian holy sites. He watched as Arabs and Jews and Catholics led millions of tourists to phony historical sites and stripped them of every financial asset they could.

On the other hand, he was dedicated to his country and his people. He loved his cultural heritage and wanted to ensure a future for his people. That's what drove him.

But had he done that? Or had he lit a fire that would ultimate destroy all that he wanted to save?

Tel Aviv

Baruch's Council-originated plan for Iran had worked! Yehuda had done his part, of course, to prompt the Cabinet and the PM to pull the trigger on 'Little Samson'. When it came to foreign threats, Mossad held all the cards of influence.

But the General prided himself on the operational strategy and the foreign players all reacting as predicted. The only real wild card was this Colonel Katz. He wasn't a council asset nor would he ever be Baruch surmised. He had carried out his orders perfectly, but his after-action report was filled with signs of suspicion concerning the relative ease of access to Fordow airspace - a precaution Baruch had arranged with Ashfin. That connection, of course, had to remain unknown, even unimagined, thus the General wondered if he was going to have a problem with Katz.

He decided to meet with the commander and determine the extent of this implied suspicion and whether or not to involve Yehuda. He planned to hold a second debriefing of the whole bombing team to cover up his true intentions and then get Katz into an off-line discussion privately. At this point, he didn't want to push the delete button on the Colonel, not unless there was a threat of exposure or of a spotlight on the operation.

A few days later, he convened the team leaders of the mission. Of course, he invited the IDF Chief of Staff Lt. Gen Eizen as per protocol for command staff back-briefings, knowing that Eizen would probably be committed to other priorities. He could credibly say the meeting was primarily for the General and then excuse all except Katz with whom he could review the after-action report.

As expected, Eizen thanked Baruch but excused himself for a meeting with the Defense Minister. So, as he entered the meeting room, he dismissed all but Yaakov who remained standing.

"Have a seat, Colonel," Baruch began. "I think we can still make the best of the time. How about a quick review of your AAR."

"Certainly, Sir," Katz removed a hardcopy from his briefing folder and then sat. "Shall I begin with 'wheels-up'?"

"I know you had to wait longer than usual for the green light, but given the seriousness of the mission, that was to be expected," the General replied. "Let's go straight the bombing run and then to the refueling."

"Yes, Sir. As planned, we used the new jamming tech over Northern Syria and Iran. Either it worked even better than predicted, much better, or we caught them totally by surprise. All teams reported very light interdiction... It was a bit strange. Very welcome, of course... but odd. The Bunker Buster basically excavated the top of the facility and created the focus crater we wanted for the nuke. Its cloud, though, was tricky to navigate as we followed fairly close with the nuke. Major Mintz and I triggered it pretty low, as planned, to minimize the blast radius. However, as a result, the shock wave hit us before we could get very far and damaged the aircraft, specifically the refueling port of the conformal tank. As a result, we only refueled enough to make it back to the Med where, as you know, we ditched."

"Good synopsis. So, you would attribute the light resistance to stealth and the new jamming capabilities?"

"That's my best guess at this point, Sir. But perhaps intel can give us further insight."

"OK, Colonel. That's all I have time for now. If I get further intelligence, I'll let you know." Baruch, of course, did not owe his subordinate that courtesy but figured that it gave him the potential reason for another discourse if necessary. He did not trust this man - too smart and too loyal. He couldn't predict whether or not he would press the observation of near-absent resistance further. He decided to wait, for the present, on involving Yehuda. Katz was too much of a secret-celebrity to eliminate him right now. But later, perhaps.

Chapter 13

Roma/Frascati

"It is interesting that the family name of this villa, Aldobrandini, literally translates to "morning star" and "falling angel", i.e., Satan," Ismail began. "And they are still one of the richest and most powerful families in the world whose ancestors include a Pope and several Cardinals. As you would imagine, they are still closely tied to the Vatican and currently tightly allied with our friend, Cardinal Parolin. That's how we acquired the unlimited use of this location. Thank you, Cardinal."

Parolin nodded to the group.

"Of course, this town, Frascati, was once home to the mother of Nero and during World War II was the General Headquarters for the Germans' Mediterranean Region. So, there's much history together with much power here which the Leader has said will work to our advantage," Ismail boasted.

The implication that the owners of this facility were potentially satanists freaked out Abdul, but as he scanned the conference room, the other Council members seemed unphased or ambivalent about it - superstitious nonsense.

Frascati is a beautiful town, southeast of Rome in the hills and is well known for its white wine. He observed that this new meeting site did provide more security for the group. In the last few months, both Cardinal Parolin and Dr. Ibrahim bin Abdul-Kareem Al-Issa had been inducted into the supremely secret organization's leadership. Along with Abdul, that made ten members.

"Let's begin with a review of operations in Iran, Ashfin," the Leader's protégé continued.

The Iranian did not discuss the bombing of Fardow. His delivery was terse and to the point. "With both Quds and Basij under my command

and my promotion to Major General, only Jefari has seniority over me. With his elimination, as well as Hajazi, it is certain that I will be called upon to be Commander in Chief of the IRGC. In light of recent events, public opinion has become one-sidedly pro-military and anti-government, so in that position I will be able to do virtually anything we decide is important."

"The state of the infrastructure?" the Saudi Prince inquired.

"As you know, the virus is extremely persistent. We can clean it in isolation, but all networked systems have proven to be repeatedly vulnerable. All internal communication is being handled by the routers formerly dedicated to our missile defense systems which we agreed I would protect from infection. It is, however, difficult to keep it that way."

For the next twenty minutes he discussed his directives from the current Iranian Chief of Staff and his intelligence on what he positioned as the government's inevitable transition and increasing dependence on military support.

Roma/Frascati

"Another success story we have to present is how powerfully persuasive our overall propaganda or communication strategy has been in the EU in particular. Prime Minister Mahgoub joined us officially a short time ago but has been under our guidance for several years now. You all know him quite well by reputation in Sudan, the UN, the Arab League and most recently, as Special Advisor to the President of the EU. He will speak to us about that program and his unique position to ensure the success of our Middle East peace initiative. Abdul?" Ismail thought of Abdul as his asset, something Yehuda secretly challenged.

Abdul felt like a lamb in the midst of a pack of wolves, but he didn't let it show. In fact, he projected a confidence that even surprised himself a bit. He used his laptop to display some data on "cultural research" conducted at his request by contracted agencies.

"All right, as you can see, we have successfully moved Europe as a whole toward the acceptance of societal change. Most countries are showing that a maximum of only 9% of the populace does not want change. With the exception of Italy and Portugal, confidence in the church is in the 20-percentile range."

"With the exception of Greece, Austria, and the UK, the migration of immigrants into Europe is being found acceptable by a large majority even as they are bringing significant influences into the culture and value systems. Also, for the first time, more than half of the population say there is no one true religion, but all great world religions are valid."

"My report contains hundreds of data points which demonstrate that we have culturally and politically turned the corner, setting the stage for our global strategies. Media partners have successfully marginalized all those who are resistant to our messages and even schools have incorporated them for reinforcement in the youth."

Abdul had previously sent his report electronically to all the members who began to study the data and as they did, smiles appeared around the room. Nevertheless, even as he sat down, Abdul felt guilty of doing a horrible thing. He'd always justified his work as ultimately right because it would eventually lead people to the true faith, but for the first time, while sensing the pleasure of this group, he seriously doubted it.

He had successfully nurtured a growing vacuum of traditional faith in the once Christian continent, all the while believing Islam would fill it. But now, his doubt quickly turned to fear that he had betrayed someone or some fundamental truth and that with this betrayal, terrible darkness was impending. His stomach churned with stress, and despite Ismail profusely praising his work, he somehow knew he had not pleased the one who really mattered.

He also realized that just as he had endeavored to change other people's values, his own were changing as well but in a different direction. He seemed to be at a crossroads internally. Nevertheless, he politely acknowledged the appreciation of the group and smiled.

"Thank you, thank you, Allah be praised," he said with the volume of his reply trailing off.

The group took a break at this point and Yehuda, ever discerning, approached.

"Are you all right, Abdul?"

"Oh yes, of course. A bit of a bad stomach, I think. I'll be fine."

Yehuda eyed him carefully and Abdul wondered if he could read his mind.

"I guess we'll tag-team this next part about the treaty, just as we planned. Will you..." the Mossad agent continued.

"Certainly, no problem. This is the best part, right?"

.

Over a decade previously, the Saudis had presented to the world a Middle East peace plan that paved the way. For the first time, an Arab country had proposed acknowledgment of the state of Israel by all Arab countries. Persian and Shi'ite Iran, of course, had vigorously belittled it. Since then the Quartet of players, Russia, the EU, the US and the UN, had struggled to present a plan to which all parties could agree.

As Special Advisor to the President and by association, the EU Parliament, Abdul had been asked to play the role of chief negotiator not only on their behalf but also as the singularly most trusted Arab representative, to bring all parties to agreement on the Peace Plan which the Council Leader and others had crafted. Thanks to Yehuda and the influence of his associates, Israel was ready to deal. Iran was vocal but making no aggressive moves at present, the US was more than ready for the generational feuding to cease. Only Russia remained a wild card, but Naryshkin's influence in Moscow on this issue was evident, and as the momentum increased towards a final agreement, the Kremlin seemed to warm to the idea.

Yehuda presented details on his behind-the-scenes work to bring Israel's cabinet to a consensus aided, of course, by the financial benefits that the US and EU pledged. Currently, the Palestinians had nearly been disenfranchised, taking a second place to the greater good of the Arab world.

With the silencing of Iran and the demonstrated willingness of Israel to deal decisively with its enemies, Hezbollah and Hamas were reigned in, at least for the time being.

In the final version, Palestinians would get some concessions, but their antagonistic leadership was effectively muzzled. Tunnels were to be filled, missiles scrapped, Israel and its regional neighbors were to scale back armaments phase by phase, all carefully defined of course, and all internationally verified, with the goal of assuring a lasting peace guaranteed by the Quartet.

Abdul deserved most of the credit, Yehuda confessed. He had been able to persuade his old friends and new acquaintances of the merits and the long-term vision. All that remained was a presentation to the UN Security Council and the General Assembly.

"At this point," the Prince interjected, "I have prepared the way among our Arab and Arab-friendly nations. The Assembly will overwhelmingly support the covenant."

"Friends, the Jews will embrace this peace without question. They will disarm, reluctantly, but they will disarm as they feel safe. And we will be ready," Ismail said with a nod to Asfin and Baruch.

Chapter 14

Tel Aviv

Yaakov sat waiting at the Cafe Birenbaum, inside at a table for two. It was a cozy place, unpretentious and a bit out of the way. In the last several days, he had noticed some tails. Today, he had shaken them, but it took quite a bit of effort. As a pilot and commander leading many classified missions even the home front was dangerous. For that reason, he was used to staying aware of his surroundings, keeping an eye out for 'followers' before and afterward.

Today's 'trackers' were evidently well trained. He longed for the days when a mission ended with the flight-deck landing, but current events had changed all that; now, in the aftermath of every mission he knew that the target on his back increased as did the surveillance. After the Fordow mission, he had discussed this with his commander but was assured that Mossad had his back.

On a lighter note, having just turned forty, his staff teased him with black balloons taped to his desk. He laughed and swore to get even. Having reached the rank of Lieutenant Colonel quickly and recently learning that he was on the short list for Colonel, he nevertheless wondered if he was cut out for what he knew lay ahead - the relentless intrigue, the endless jeopardy, the lack of personal relationships. His drive and sense of purpose were undiminished, but in these moments of silent musing he recognized a longing, a hunger for something more than what had motivated him previously.

He sprinkled salt in the olive oil in front of him.

His attention snapped back to the front as he noticed Captain Mintz enter the cafe and approach his table. In her off-duty attire, she could turn every head. Yaakov was attracted to her instantly and wondered why he had not really noticed her beauty before. Her eyes sparkled even as she maintained her professional demeanor. Katz was so entirely devoted to his work, he rarely dated, let alone pursued a deeper relationship. But, in this moment he felt differently. Something sparked in his heart.

She took the seat across from him and smiled with a hint of embarrassment, noticing the look in his eyes.

"Have you been waiting long?" she started.

"No, but I have been looking forward to our meeting. Would you like something to drink?" He motioned to the bartender behind him.

"Sure," she replied demurely. "And Colonel…"

"Please, we're off duty. Call me Yaakov."

"Yaakov," she smiled warmly, "I've anticipated this as well. General Baruch, well I hate to say it, but he makes me nervous, and I almost feel dirty after talking with him. Sounds insubordinate I guess."

"Don't worry, you're not alone and not on record," Yaakov said with empathy. "My superiors are respectful of his record and operational skills, but they say it's almost too good. You know, in confidence, I'll tell you it wouldn't surprise me to learn that there are a closet full of skeletons in his background."

"And his eyes…" she caught herself and decided not to finish the thought.

"What about his eyes?" Yaakov queried.

"Oh, I don't know if it's worth mentioning, but they're not just hard, or lustful… they're suspicious. I mean, I feel like he could be nice one instant and then put me on a hit list the next. I can't help but feel like he thinks I know too much about something I shouldn't."

"Do you?" Yaakov asked calmly and without insinuation.

Tamar was quiet for several seconds, then offered, "Of course. It's part of my job. But with him, I'm not talking about information that's just top-secret. Rather something bigger, something that's not even classified or known by the government. It's just a feeling of sorts. Nothing specific."

"Do you feel like you're in danger?"

"Umm, maybe. But again, it's just a feeling. I need to talk with my sister. I know that doesn't sound very professional, but she is amazing. I turn to her when I sense I'm in trouble and she knows exactly what to say and do," Tamar explained.

"No, no. Not at all. I don't have anyone like that. Wish I did," Yaakov answered. "In fact..." now he paused but then decided to test the waters. "... I'd like to see if you and I could get to know each other more. I hope I'm not being 'unprofessional' myself. I want to..."

"I would like that," she interrupted and gently touched his hand. Her eyes looked into his.

Yaakov's hardened heart sprang to life. Never, ever, ever, had he felt this way before. He quietly gasped and thought some sort of an explosion had taken place inside. It was several seconds before he recovered.

"Tamar, you know, I'm thinking that I've probably got ten years on you. You realize that, right?"

She feigned surprise and then chuckled. "I'd never have guessed, Colonel. You're in great shape for your age."

Despite the excitement of a potential new relationship, both of them had Baruch in the back of their minds. Such a powerful man, even his superiors treaded carefully around him. If his career continued as it had, it wasn't difficult to imagine him as running all the IDF and perhaps more. Was that his goal? Were Yaakov and Tamar somehow just obstacles to that end?

Or, was the questioning associated with the AAR all about something else? And again, why did he want to know so much about Yaakov's opinion of why there was so little opposition at Fordow? Yaakov could report it but other than that, he could only guess as to why. The General knew that. Why was he so inquisitive on that point? He didn't seem to care about the damaged refueling port or the loss of the aircraft over the Med.

Tamar was alarmed by the character she seemed to see in Baruch. She honestly thought he was capable of anything and his interest in her was not the science of data, that much was clear. He gave her the creeps. Maybe it was simply a sexual turn-off for her, but she also sensed that he was covering something up, something that if exposed would come back on him.

"So, what are we going to do about our 'man of the hour'?" Yaakov posed.

"I'm not sure. We should both avoid him when possible. If he's dirty somehow, he's also brilliant and we don't have any proof yet of any wrongdoing."

"Should we ask around? I have friends…" as Yaakov considered this his voice trailed off. The last thing he wanted was to endanger Tamar. "No… no, forget it… not in this environment. Little Samson is a big coup for him, and no one is going to want to expose anything on him right now. Let's not discuss this with anyone else… except your sister of course if you want to. But even her – tell her to keep it to herself."

"I agree. I think it all may pass over and surely there are now huge issues, international issues, hanging over all of us." Tamar gripped his hand. "And I'm glad we've gotten together. You make me feel safer."

Tel Aviv

Tamar looked in the mirror at home and for few moments pondered what it was that Yaakov saw in her, and what she'd notice in him that clicked, that electrified their meeting earlier. To be sure, he was handsome and strong. But beyond the looks, he obviously had a heart that she could touch. He wasn't the ice-cold jet-jock she'd heard about. It was obvious he thought she was beautiful, but there was definitely more going on in him.

She had spent her youth in the Long Island burbs of New York until her family moved to Israel when she was ten. Growing up, her older sister and she were wild, and though their parents parked them on a kibbutz for months at a time, they didn't discover their work ethic. Rather, they discovered work-arounds, skirting the rules and ending up in trouble. They even ditched the 'butz' and 'hitch-hiked' a plane ride to England on El Al to get to a concert but had to pan-handle for the money to get back.

But when her sister met her husband at a meeting for messianic Jews in London, it shocked her and drove her away from home and family for years. She felt betrayed and became angry and isolated until she realized her gift for understanding systems and mathematics.

Moving to Haifa, she graduated at the very top of her class in Technion. That, combined with her two year conscription in the military gave her a radical realignment of personal priorities. Wildness turned to devotion for her country while rebellion gave way to rationalism and scientific inquiry.

At the same time, she loved the notion of artistic creativity and frequently found herself in galleries and flirtatiously involved with men who shared that same interest. There was never any serious relationship though, and when she ran into trouble, emotional or professional, she turned to her sister for support. At first, that was difficult as in her own mind, there was chasm between them. Essa's new faith was the issue. However, in time, Tamar found her love for her sister revived and even enhanced somehow.

She pulled out her phone and dialed the international call. Essa had last emailed her from Rome. There was no answer, so she left a message, "It's me. I need to share something with you, actually, a couple of things. I've met someone, and no, he's not a painter. And I've got a more sobering deal going on at work. Please call me today if you can. Love you."

It was a couple of weeks later that she really got concerned about her work. In studying the data intercepts from Iran, she found one, then two, highly encrypted messages from an IDF IP address to an Iranian military address. They were sent just prior to the Little Samson mission. And then she found several more, moving between one Iranian military IP and another during the time when all communication was supposed to be, and had been reported to be, down due to her team's Pan malware.

Decryption was one of her specialties, and though it took considerable effort, she discovered the keys. What she uncovered shocked her.

"LS is a go. Evacuate F and stand down per plan," read the message to someone in the IRG. The source was someone at Dimona. LS had to be Little Samson and F was Fardow she surmised. Her heart nearly beat audibly as she realized the implications. The mission's security was not only compromised but apparently coordinated with the IRG. How high did this go? Who could she trust? How much more was there going on that obviously endangered the IDF and Israel as a whole?

Unknown to Tamar was the extent of corruption at the highest levels made by Baruch and the bottomless pockets of the Council over decades. It wasn't that the entire senior staff had sold out their country. But money speaks to many people and especially when it's combined with threats and 'professional consequences'- the proverbial carrot and stick.

Baruch had many who were afraid of him and many who were receptive to his ideas based on financial enhancement. Like the Chinese and the Americans, his fellow Israelis had always had a penchant for the pursuit of wealth and the General knew it well. He spent covertly and lavishly on nurturing his network of associates. As a consequence, he could do far more than a General of his rank by simply making a call.

He basically 'owned' over 170 senior personnel in both military and governmental positions along with their 'resources'. Of course, he and

Yehuda competed in this, but the assassin's network was both within the nation and in many countries abroad. 'Unfair advantage', Baruch mused, knowing his associate had far greater reach.

Chapter 15

Mexico City

The two bell towers and 25 bells of the Mexico City Metropolitan Cathedral seemed to all be ringing at once. In the Plaza de la Constitution, Zocalo, as it's called, were gathered well over 100,000 people cheering, weeping, yelling, all in a dizzying melee - a sea of devoted humanity. Often a place of political protest, it better resembled now a hub of human frenzy stretching out in all directions. Every boulevard, avenue and street was packed to capacity with people - perhaps a million, all waiting to hear from their beloved visitor, Pope Gregory X.

As he emerged from the Cathedral, amid a swarm of guards, and took his place behind the bullet-proof shield protecting the lectern, he then stepped back and took several minutes to bless many in the crowd. This agitated his security detail who carefully eyed the surrounding host, pushing some away.

The high-ranking government officials present on the stage, together with Cardinal Carrero, Cardinal Parolin and Archbishop Retas stood and hailed the Prelate for his kind efforts. Meanwhile, snipers by the hundreds surrounded the plaza. Zocalo was a powder-keg of enthusiasm.

Slowly, he disengaged from the crowd and made his way back to the podium. With Spanish being his native tongue, he nevertheless opened by welcoming everyone in multiple languages and the oceans of people hushed.

Suddenly, before he could go any further, a man broke through the barriers protecting the stage and before security guards could stop him, he shot three times at the Pope. Gregory fell to the ground and was immediately enclosed by his security team. The gunman, a middle eastern man, tried to run but the crowds had no mercy. Before the police could intervene, he was a dead bloody mess.

Several minutes passed during which time the crowds were strangely silent. Then, as though resurrected from the dead, the Pope arose and went immediately to the podium, right arm raised, and the crowds exploded in such noise that the buildings around the plaza shook.

As if nothing had happened, he spoke of the need to be a light in the darkness, to embrace neighbors near and from afar, to protect the planet and to worship God, eschewing materialism. His talk was briefer than usual while he appeared to favor his left side. As he stepped back down, the unthinkable happened. A bomb exploded in front of the Cathedral bringing down part of the restored facade and burying dozens of people. The streets were too packed for emergency vehicles and tragically hundreds, perhaps thousands, were trampled and killed. None of those on the stage were hurt but they all made a hasty exit into highly secure vehicles. Meanwhile the Pope, the Cardinals and the Archbishop were helicoptered away to an unknown location.

For weeks afterward, the papers sought to publish answers as to how it all could have happened. They lambasted the police, the government and even the Pope and his staff for placing so many in harm's way. Despite his own wounds, Gregory was ultimately portrayed by the press as more of a culprit than a victim. His leadership was questioned, and some took it as an opportunity to challenge the church as a whole.

Aboard AZ4000 over the Atlantic

Immediately after the tragedy

Shepherd One, as it's called, streamed its way back to Italy with both the Pope and his senior Cardinal aboard. Gregory was wounded in his left arm in the attack, Parolin was unscathed.

"Your Holiness, this is now the second attempt on your life in as many years. The previous time, it was a sniper and we lost Archbishop..." the Cardinal engaged.

"You needn't remind me, Joseph. Tragic times, to be sure, and no amount of security can protect us perfectly," the Pope interjected.

"But you saw the numbers. Over eighteen hundred killed, more than five thousand injured. The Church has suffered a great disaster. What are you going to do?" Parolin was carefully inserting a verbal scalpel and preparing to twist it. The Prelate was two years older than his predecessor who had been the first Pope in a long time to step down. Gregory was old but not unaware of the Cardinal's ambition or methods. He could see the question as being intended to force his hand, to commit to a course of action without council. And, it wasn't the first time Parolin had tried to do this.

"Joseph, I am not prepared to do anything just yet. I need more information about what broke down. The Mexican government and federal police are not going to welcome any unilateral statement or actions before they have had time to do their own investigations. You of all people must be sensitive to that."

"Of course, but I'm not referring to just the attacks. Your policy decisions are being seen by more and more as disruptive and incongruent with canon. And so, how do we know these attacks are from the outside?"

"You're suggesting some from within our own house would try to kill me??"

"I'm reminding you, Your Holiness, of what you already know; that your decrees and policy changes have introduced significant discord. Together with the appearance of tolerance for sexual offenses..."

"You know there is no tolerance, just forgiveness with repentance."

"That is not the optics. In any event, you have made enemies within and without. And, it is crumbling our efforts to emphasize common ground with the splinter churches and other faiths. Within our House, there are many who are speaking to me to persuade you to consider following Pope Benedict. They are questioning your ability to lead in these increasingly stressful times."

"I am aware. And just what do you think, Joseph?"

The Cardinal paused. This was the moment that would define his future and the future of the entire Church, no, rather the entire world. He knew exactly how he would put it.

"Your Holiness, you must decide. However, I do notice signs of... well, a digression so to speak. Forgetfulness, increased frustration and anger. You know I support you, but..." now the twist of the blade, "the longer you remain on the thrown the greater the disarray in the Church, and the Kingdom itself is damaged. I know you could not live with that on your conscience."

Gregory at first looked angry and then a forlorn appearance came over him. Parolin left. The discussion ended when he hung his head in prayer and indecision. Two hours later, he murmured to himself, "You may be right, Joseph. You may be right."

Roma

Ten days later, Gregory called for a conference of senior Vatican leaders as well as trustworthy Cardinals. Parolin was invited. The Pope offered to them his petition for retirement and after several minutes of uncertain awkward silence, they began to discuss the necessary process. Groups formed in the chamber according to myriad priorities and preferences. Although it was not the College of Cardinals, many spoke of who the next Pope should or could be.

Unknown to Parolin, the Council had been preparing for this for years and so, of course, when he heard his own name floated frequently in the chambers, his vanity caused him to presume it was of his own doing. Some even asked him what his priorities would be should he be elected.

"Of course, there are many issues to address, but unity must be our top priority, unity within and a push for much greater unity worldwide," he answered. No one imagined the extent to which he intended that unity to spread. No one other than the Leader.

Nearly three months later, white smoke from the tiny chimney atop the Sistine Chapel announced the new Pope. Parolin would change his name.

Chapter 16

The large conference hall was empty save for the eight people meeting at the central table. Translators weren't needed. Abdul had been here many times before but never in his present capacity. Across from him were the senior-most representatives of Syria, Egypt, Jordan, Saudi Arabia and to his side those from Iraq, Libya and Sudan. With the exception of the Sudanese, he had maintained exceedingly good relationships with all of them over many years and was held in the highest regard. This core group represented the interests of most of the Muslim world.

"My friends, final policy sessions with the Quartet are scheduled for tomorrow. In the past year, I have actively engaged each of you to address how we achieve a just and stable outcome, a lasting peace in the Middle East. You know that you can trust me to be honest with you and to verify all commitments around this table as well as those represented at tomorrow's. I'm very happy to say that your concerns… and demands… have been reasonably accommodated by Israel, the EU and the US, while Russia and China are willing to support the decision of the General Assembly. Our Palestinian brothers have also realized that their interests are being represented and have asked me to reaffirm your commitment to their welfare. They also will abide by this newest agreement."

Abdul believed that his efforts on the international treaty were just. At the same time, he knew the 'eyes' of the Council were upon him. The document, as it stood presently, had begun with the old Saudi proposal. More recently, it had been resurrected by the Prince, embellished by the US and EU, then was tirelessly negotiated and tuned by Abdul. It was finally edited and approved by the Council's Leader. Abdul knew he was simply the 'mouthpiece' of the Council's work behind the scenes. Even the Quartet had been drawn into their net. Israel was thrilled with the potential of a lasting peace and final recognition of their rights and security. All but a few were tired of war and threats of war. In addition, the promise of financial benefits for all signatories, both short and long term, were staggering and being borne primarily by the EU and US.

On the surface, the treaty seemed promising. The ultimate goal, however, of the Council remained hidden from the public, even Abdul.

"Now, we have rehearsed the articles in this agreement exhaustively to the point that we should be able to confirm our willingness to support and promote it. I'm confident..."

"Mr. Mahgoub," the Sudanese official interrupted, refusing to address Abdul as Prime Minister, "I only have one remaining issue. How will your work during the last three years, and your international reputation, influence your ambitions in my country? Are you planning to return?"

"That is off-topic, Asim," the Saudi prince interjected.

"And it can be discussed, if necessary, off-line," added the Iraqi.

Both men were Council members. At this point, Abdul knew that if the Sudanese pressed the issue further, he would likely never make it back to his country.

"Mr. Prime Minister," Abdul was gracious in using his countryman's new title, "I understand your concern, but our colleagues' comments are indeed appropriate for this meeting. So... I'm going to ask each of you to sign this cover page. Copies will be distributed within the hour."

Everyone signed including Asim.

New York, UN, Office of Deputy Secretary General Aafia Mohammed, a covert Council asset

"And so, we will finally be granted acknowledgment of our state. And we will, at last, be justly compensated for the suffering of our people." Abbal, anticipating the arrival of PM Mahgoub, spoke to his Palestinian delegation.

"But can we really trust..." his deputy started to ask.

"We can and will trust our partners, not the Jews. Not yet. We will trust our brothers and our allies. And I trust Mahgoub," the Palestinian leader interjected.

"It seems like we have no choice. The new alliances with Iran, Iraq, the Kurds, the Turks and Syria... and Russia. This is our only bet, our only potentially positive outcome," said the Hamas representative. "Since they dropped the bomb on Fardow, concern for our claims have all but vanished. Everyone is suddenly backing away from us."

Abdul then entered the office and took a seat next to Abbal.

"Good news, my brothers, the entire forum of Muslim Unity has endorsed the plan to compensate you and protect you with international support. You will be recognized, finally, as you should be." Looking around the room, he knew what was on their minds.

"Words on paper are on thing, my brother, and we are glad for them. But we are looking to you to ensure that all parties to this agreement follow through," replied Abbal for all of them.

It was the Quartet that was taking credit for the breakthroughs. However, most understood that the nuke had demonstrated Israel's resolve which ultimately brought all parties to the table. And, the reality was that Abdul had been the key to the treaty negotiations and final draft status.

Consequently, he felt the weight of the world, almost literally, on his shoulders.

"I completely understand, my brothers," he replied.

Of course, Abdul did not relate to his Palestinian friends simply at arm's length or theoretically. His own country had been ruled by the British and over-lorded by the Egyptians and more recently was a target of the Russians. He himself had always been fiercely devoted to independence and Sudanese sovereignty. He considered their association with, and at times manipulation by the terrorists as unhealthy for their state and fundamentally counter to their aspirations.

He knew their history well – not their history books, but the whole story, and he cared for them. For generations, their people were used as the 'point of the spear' in the Muslim counter to the Jews after failing miserably to use their own military force. 'So much pointless death on both sides fueled by irrational anger and vengeance,' he thought.

Abdul was African, his wife was Arabic. But as a Muslim he related to them and honestly strove to bring them peace – a peace they could use to build their society apart from hatred. It was going to take a shift or rather a complete change of course for them – one that meant discarding decades of teaching and preaching of hatred and victimhood. And as he considered this, it hit him hard –

Like them, he himself was facing a personal decision, an impending crisis of choice. In the back of his mind, the contrast was becoming clearer and his need to decide more poignant.

New York

The Muslim Unity nations had signed; the Palestinians had signed. Tomorrow he anticipated the Quartet representatives would sign and then finally, he would deal again with the Israeli Prime Minister and his Cabinet. It was indeed a momentous time for the Middle East and Abdul had worked tirelessly in every capital to bring consensus on a dilemma that plagued the region for generations.

Abdul had long been involved with the endless chaos of the Middle East. As a fervent Muslim, his position had always been whole heartedly against the State of Israel but over time - literally years of negotiations between Islamic heads of state, at the UN and most recently on behalf of the EU, he knew that neither side had a righteous cause. He became convinced that even a temporary peace, let alone a lasting one had to include all Arab Muslim governments and would fundamentally boil down to money and security.

He also knew he would have to draw upon every personal and professional relationship he had to find a non-wavering buy in. Ultimately, it was the terrorist organizations who rejected every overture and who Abdul came down against. He informed the Council of their intransigence and not long afterward, their leaders started dropping – mysterious assassinations or accidents. It didn't take long for the remaining leadership to get the message that cooperation was in their best interest.

Abdul was never heavy handed and was shocked as he noticed the consequences of his Council reports on the Treaty. Nevertheless, elimination of the key obstacles proved effective. At that point, he worked with the US, EU and Saudis to construct an evergreen compensation program that addressed not only the greed of the principle players but development of schooling, healthcare, infrastructure and more.

The next piece was the most difficult, security not by the build-up of massive amounts of armaments as had always been the assumed solution, but a gradual disarmament, mostly of the WMDs throughout the

Middle East. Peace through strength simply could not work in the region. Arabs had bioweapons and missiles, Israel had those and nukes. In addition, security had to be audited and enforced by 'the world' – i.e. the UN and strongly backed by every world power.

The crowning achievement, however, was the notion of religious tolerance reflected in the Arab nations allowing a portion of the temple mount in Jerusalem to be allocated to Israel and to be used only for religious purposes. Both sides agreed that worshipping a single Creator would allow for that compromise.

That evening, he hit his pillow and slept hard. However, in the early morning he had a startlingly realistic dream in which he sat at a cafe drinking sweet tea in a large cup. A beautiful woman approached, sat at the table with him and tipped the teacup over. The tea spilled out on the ground and suddenly a vine began to emerge from where it had spilled. The plant at first appeared interesting to Abdul, then startling, as it wound around him, then he realized he was one with the vine and he felt a peace like nothing he'd ever experienced.

Waking up, his frame of mind was strangely joyful. After dressing and going over his notes for the day, he left to get some breakfast. The hotel restaurant was the logical choice, but as he neared it, he thought he would try something different and exited. He walked a block to Second Avenue and then turned and went up to 44th Street. There, he found John's Coffee Shop. Inside, he took a seat at the booth for two situated against the partition and ordered some tea.

Just a few moments later, a very beautiful woman, possibly Jewish, came in and looked around the Cafe as if searching for someone. Evidently, not seeing whoever she was looking for, she sat at a table quite near Abdul and set her case on the floor next to her. Abdul suddenly felt a 'deja vu'.

"Excuse me, Miss, it appears like the person you're expecting is not here yet. Would you like some company while you wait?"

She thought for a bit and then shrugged, "Sure, why not? You seem harmless," she said and smiled at him. But as she sat down opposite him, she looked a little surprised, "Wait a minute! Aren't you Mahgoub, I mean

Prime Minister Mahgoub with the EU? I've been keeping up with your work in the news."

Abdul was embarrassed and pleasantly surprised himself. "Yes, yes. But I am rarely recognized in this country. Your accent tells me you are perhaps Israeli?"

"I am. By the way, my name's Tamar. I'm visiting today and will be observing, for my government, the UN Plenary on Middle East Cooperation. Aren't you involved though?"

"I'm afraid I cannot discuss that, but perhaps you can offer your own ideas on the Plenary. Or maybe just tell me a little about yourself."

"Oh, not much to tell really. I'm a bit of a data nut so to speak." She picked up the menu and asked, "Would you like to order something?"

"Of course."

A couple of minutes later, they had both ordered.

"Prime Minister, I've noted by reading the papers that you seem to be on the road a lot. Do you have a family? Pardon me if I'm being too personal…"

"No, not at all. Yes, I do. A wonderful family, however, I haven't seen them in a long time - so much work. But how about you?"

"No. No one special yet," she answered and waited a few seconds. "I have a sister I miss tremendously though. She lives in Athens right now."

"Athens? That's curious. I was thinking you remind me of someone I know in Athens. Do you perchance, have a photo?"

She opened the photo gallery on her phone and showed him a picture of her sister. Abdul's eyes opened wide and he exclaimed, "Vanessa! You're Vanessa's sister? I can hardly believe it. I have missed her and James so much."

At this point, Tamar was completely surprised as well. "It's amazing that you know them! I had lost touch with her for a couple of years and then just a few weeks ago, I felt like I had to talk with her again. Someone in my work who is really good at finding people got me her new phone number and we reconnected. You know obviously, we are Jewish, but she became a Messianic Jew when she met James and she has shared her faith with me frequently. I always blew it off, for a lot of reasons, but when we shared together again just recently, I just knew what she was telling me was true. I mean, it has altered my perspectives and ..." she caught herself. "Mr Prime Minister, I apologize. I didn't mean to be so forward."

"No need to be concerned, Tamar. They have shared extensively with me as well. Between you and me, I almost find myself like you. I think that what they have lived out in front of me and what they have shared are both like seeds that are planted in my heart. And something good is growing though I cannot yet say what. But I am seeing things differently as well."

"You know, as a Jew, I was always told that we should not trust Christians and that they were responsible for all sorts of terrible things done to my people," Tamar said with her face turning downward.

"I can relate to that," Abdul offered. "But I don't think it's that simple now. I think we have to understand that some people claim to be this or that and in truth, they are just faking it. They are simply using the faith and those who believe it for their own ends."

"And some are the real deal," she responded looking Abdul in the eye. "Nessa says when God's truth is planted in good 'heart-soil' it bears his fruit."

"What's good heart-soil?" he asked.

"She says it varies from person to person and only God knows the heart, but often it is related to brokenness and humility, kind of like a farmer who breaks up the earth before planting."

Abdul nodded and pondered that point. That sounded familiar, like something James had said.

"Well, that gives me more to ponder. Allah has brought difficulty into my own life."

"Maybe it was Christ's Spirit."

Abdul was a little surprised by her suggestion. He was prone to interpret the truthful things he heard through the filter of Islam and to disregard whatever didn't fit his understanding. This, however, was a bullseye on his heart and potentially answered one of his long-held questions.

"I must consider that," he said and smiled.

He was taken with the innocence and newness of Tamar's joy. 'Just like her sister,' he mused.

"Can I pray for you?" she said and slightly gasped, surprising herself with the question. "You know, I've never even considered asking anyone that. I apologize if it offended you," she said boldly and then shyly.

Abdul looked hard in her eyes and somehow knew he should agree. "Of course, my dear."

She lightly held his hand and prayed a simple prayer for his protection and insight.

"Can you pray for my family also?" Abdul was now the one who was surprised by his own request.

Her prayer continued fluidly and as though it was the expression of some power within her. Afterward, Abdul thought perhaps he should now file this experience mentally into the 'simple courtesy' folder so to speak. Nevertheless, as they parted, heading off into the stress filled day, he was glad for it and hoped he could one day soon talk with James about it all.

Chapter 17

New York

This was a day he had rued for quite some time. The bullet proof Escalade took him to the front round-about drive of an estate having at least a score of armed guards. The grounds were expansive and landscaped exquisitely. Abdul had rarely seen, at least in the US, such an overstated expression of secured opulence. Driving past the guarded gates and on to the mansion took three to four minutes. He noted the sniper towers disguised as trees and the seemingly hundreds of cameras. Exiting the vehicle, he was escorted promptly to a rear entrance and found himself going up in an elevator to the roof. At that point, he was led to a waiting helicopter, strapped in, and given headphones. As the chopper rose, the pilot looked back at Abdul and said, "Don't be alarmed, sir."

He flipped a couple of switches and the entire aircraft went dark inside.

"Is this the new Israeli transparency tech? I heard it was in test." Abdul asked. There was no answer.

The flight lasted about thirty minutes in which all he could see were the lights on the instrumentation panels. The pilot was apparently flying by way of a virtual reality screen. Upon touch-down, the side door opened to four armed guards who motioned for him to exit. Upon doing so, he glanced back and saw only the darkened interior of the helicopter through the open door. A guard shut the door and the aircraft went completely invisible again.

Obviously, he was on the roof of some skyscraper with a 360-degree view of New York, but he didn't know which one. Without ceremony or delay, he was escorted inside and taken to a top floor corner office as large as an entire suite. As he entered, the windows darkened to the point that the single occupant of the room was barely visible. The guards left and he noted the door locked as they did so.

A few moments of awkward silence passed while Abdul thought he saw the other person take a seat.

"Your eyes will adjust, my friend. Have a seat with me. We have some important items to discuss."

Abdul moved carefully to the sofa opposite his host. As he did so, the other man adjusted the lights slightly brighter.

"Better?"

"Thank you, Sir. Yes."

"Mahgoub, I am not disappointed with my investment in you. Ismail tells me you are tireless and gifted - apparently so. When you first came to my attention, you were an aimless, angry young man, devoted to your faith but needing direction. And now, here you are, at the pinnacle of your talents - bringing the world together, the confidant of so many important leaders and trusted by my Council."

Abdul wanted to respond but felt unable. He nodded to the Leader.

"Respectful as well. Very good. Now, tell me about the follow up to our treaty."

Suddenly, Abdul felt his tongue loosened. "Sir, as you well know, the treaty is only the first step to peace. Our communication strategy transitions now to ensuring Israeli disarmament. You know, there are a few Jewish leaders who will not tolerate that."

"Yes, we're taking care of them."

"So... since it is imperative that the Jews feel safe, I've prepared a series of messages targeting Shi'ites, Sunnis, Jews and the... wretched ones...," he swallowed hard. He could no longer think of the Christians like James and Vanessa in that way, "that we will flood into all our media channels. This will include key statements issued by select governments and UN officials which will positively portray the imperative of peaceful disarmament and the rapid progress, regardless, together with the overall polls showing an increasing sense of safety."

"Acceptable. The Pan virus, is it persisting?"

"Yes, even more than expected. Of course, that works to our advantage as Iran cannot use its missiles, nor can Hezbolah. Even the Russians are reduced to lower tech defense systems for now while they continue to contain it. The Saudis are essentially grounded as well."

"Excellent, Mahgoub. As our Minister of Information, I'm going to give you now some additional insight."

The Leader leaned closer and Abdul felt a thickness in his throat. His heart began to fill with a sense of fear until, to his surprise, he flashed upon the memory of little Tasha - her face, so radiant with joy. For some reason, the fear dissipated, and his throat cleared.

"I will soon take the reins of the EU myself," the Leader seemed to whisper, "as well as NATO, which we will turn into an overwhelming military force. You are to prepare the necessary media blitz to set up the denigration of these three European leaders," he handed Abdul an envelope. "Ismail will let you know when to launch it. In addition, you're going to negotiate and organize a new alliance - one we have been nurturing for decades, but which needs a catalyst soon to accomplish our goals. I think you can handle the additional multitasking, right?"

"Of course," he replied, but his voice was shaking.

"One last thing, my friend. It seems like you have spent quite a bit of time with a couple of Americans in Athens. Can they be useful? Are they trustworthy?" At this, Abdul noticed a slight hiss in the Leader's voice.

"Sir, they are only acquaintances who share my likes in music. They are harmless, but they are excellent people..."

"I see. I sssee. I must meet them sometime. That is all. You may go now."

As he left the office, Abdul was definitely shaken and felt he had somehow betrayed his friends. He also knew that they could never meet this powerful man. He'd never let that happen.

New York

Later that same day, Abdul learned that he no longer needed to meet with the Quartet representatives as an envelope was delivered to his room securely which contained the signed cover page of the treaty. The UN, the EU, Russia and the US had all endorsed the treaty. A note was attached.

"We're almost there, my friend. My gift. Now, you must finish this with the Jews."

Abdul knew who had sent it. Immediately, he called his assistant to reschedule a meeting with the Israeli PM and FM who were both in New York for special UN meetings. The plenary session was on the calendar in two days. Even though the signing of the cover page was basically a rubber stamp at this point, the formality showed good faith in advance of the global initiative. After the signatories ratified the Treaty, there would be a final confirmation process. Fortunately, the two Israelis made accommodation and agreed to meet Abdul the next day.

That evening after another lonely dinner, he texted James, "Can we talk? I can call you."

A few minutes later, an answer, "Sure."

At 1:00 AM, Abdul made the call. It was 8:00 AM in Athens.

Vanessa answered, "Is that you, Abdul?"

"My dear, yes. How good to hear your voice! You will never guess who I met the day before yesterday, here in New York."

"I think I can," she said cheerfully. "You met my sister! What a crazy small world! She let me know right away. I was surprised she was in New York."

"That's right. And what a pleasant time we had. She is delightful!"

"Did she tell you of the change in her heart?"

"Yes, she did. And I have to tell you, something is changing in me as well. We can talk more about that when I get back to Europe. Is James there too?"

"Yes, he's here. I'll put you on speaker."

Abdul wasn't sure how to relay that he might have endangered them. He paused for several seconds.

"Abdul, are you there?"

"Yes, yes, I've been missing you both and thinking quite a bit about what you've shared with me. In fact, little Tasha kind of saved me recently."

"Tasha? What do you mean? No, sweetheart, Daddy's talking to someone on the phone, not you."

"Well it was actually the memory I have of her. I'll tell you more later. However, I want to share something with you that you must treat as highly, highly confidential." He waited.

"Okay, Abdul. Something EU-ish?"

"All I can say is that I'm involved with a highly secret group that wields unimaginable power world-wide. The new peace treaty in the Middle East is essentially their work and I have been their ambassador."

"You're kidding! That's beyond prophetic! Do you realize what you've accomplished? I mean, it's in the Bible, Abdul. You are involved in fulfilling ancient prophecy. We really do need to talk when you return."

Abdul was taken aback. He had never really read the Christian scriptures and was shocked to be somehow involved with their fulfillment.

"James, Vanessa. I'm humbled and honestly, I don't know what to think but I trust you both completely. What I accidentally did this morning... what I mean is... I hope I haven't put you in jeopardy..."

"What are you saying? I've never heard you tongue-tied before," James replied.

"The man who leads this group is frighteningly powerful and he asked about my relations with you. I only told him you were very good people and very trustworthy. But he considers all Christians as "the wretched". I've seen people disappear for even questioning him, so now, I'm worried about you."

"Abdul, you are so kind to think of us. We've always expected to wear a bullseye for our faith. We don't want trouble but if it comes, we are prepared."

"You are? Are you armed?" Abdul asked sincerely.

"In a manner of speaking, yes."

Abdul was relieved. 'They must have some protection I don't know about,' he thought.

"Abdul, is your family all right?" Vanessa asked.

"I believe so. Aziz tells me they all have left Khartoum, but I don't know where they are right now. Please... please pray for them." For the first time, he felt no awkwardness in seeking help from their God.

"Absolutely! Love you, Abdul."

He hung up, knowing the line was secure. At least, he'd been told it was.

"Do you think we should be concerned? Abdul wouldn't say those things if he wasn't worried," Vanessa asked her husband.

"What can I say. He's told us next to nothing about his work or his associates. I see his name in the papers occasionally, but we don't know anything for sure. Where are the kids?"

"Outside. Michael's climbing an olive tree and Tasha is upset she can't reach the lower branch yet." Vanessa was a bit anxious despite James calm demeanor, but she chuckled at the sight of Tasha jumping up and down just missing the tree limb while her brother teased her from above.

Both of them sat and prayed again for Abdul and his family. It was a heart-felt prayer. Then James went outside and lifted Tasha up to where Michael was. She swatted Michael and laughed, "I'm higher than you are," then quickly said, "Daddy, don't let go! It's scary up here."

A moment later they were all three on the ground, wrestling, tickling and laughing excitedly. Watching that, Vanessa let the warnings from Abdul fade away.

Chapter 18

Roma

Yehuda was once again in disguise, waiting for Parolin. The difference now was that he was waiting for a Pope. Almost every second of the day was planned out and widely observed for the new Pontiff. As a result, he could no longer attend Council meetings in Frascati. Yehuda's undercover skills, his tradecraft, exceeded those of the other members and thus, it fell to him to meet, when needed, face to face with Parolin, now known as Pope Pietro.

No more meetings in dark remote chambers or some distant location, everything was done in plain sight. This time, as the Pope's bodyguard, they could converse between Parolin's stops and today they had no more than five minutes.

"Mossad." The Pope approached Yehuda who was in disbelief, thinking his cover was being blown.

"What?!" he said in as controlled a manner as possible thinking he was going to break Parolin's neck.

As they both got into the sound proof section of the Pope's limo, he continued.

"I said, Mossad. I'm going to pin the assassination attempt on Mossad. It is the Leader's directive. Of course, we will wait for the right time, but we will need to coordinate responses immediately with Ashfin and Naryshkin. Ismail is busy with EU 'business' so you will need to handle two things quickly. First, be prepared to identify the 'rogue' agents that are to blame in your directorate and also make sure Mahgoub broadcasts a sympathetic and compelling media message so that public opinion becomes overwhelmingly anti-Israeli. Rabin must be cornered publicly and pressured internally to appease world opinion."

The Israeli Prime Minister, having recently endorsed the Unity Peace Plan at the UN, was still balking a bit in demilitarizing northern Israel. He was dragging he feet.

The highly skilled assassin despised this new Council member telling him what to do. He could contain his anger but consoled himself thinking he would one day have the Leader's permission to end this whole church business. For now, he surmised that the Leader was simply using this actor.

"Understood," Yehuda did not elaborate.

The car soon stopped, and the Prelate exited leaving his 'bodyguard' inside. Several others took his place as the Pope was immediately surrounded by adoring worshipers and clergy. The limo departed, stopping again a couple of blocks further and the Israeli got out.

What the Pope did not know was that Yehuda's Council assets were already working with Ismail to eliminate the 'obstructions' in Europe. This was the EU 'business.' Under the circumstances, simple assassinations wouldn't work. That's why Ismail was running the op. Yehuda's next stop was Tel Aviv, but first a secure text to Moscow...

Yehuda had dealt with the SVR Director several times recently. Though he respected Yehuda's reputation, Naryshkin always 'fact-checked' information coming from the Council. His untraceable message was sent directly to the Russian's phone and required a thumbprint to open. The device was one of the few allowed to operate in the Moscow Pan-phobia environment.

"D proceeds. A will contact. Tell P you will not face n. M will take a hit on V," it read.

Naryshkin knew D stood for Dreamworks, A was Ashfin, P was his boss, n meant nukes, M was Mossad. V, he was not sure, but presumed to mean Vatican since the Mexican assassination was recent.

With most tech in the military still being purged from the ultra-persistent Pan virus and isolated away from networks with potential contamination. The Russians were not in an aggressive mode. On the other hand, although civil defense systems were crippled, nuclear defense systems were on the highest alert. Of course, the US and the Chinese were well aware of this and had made sure that no actions on their part would be misinterpreted. It was, however, a convenient time for Russia to begin to posture troop movement as precautionary in a time of vulnerability and no one wanted to rile a wounded bear so to speak.

Naryshkin decided to initiate contact himself. He sent a secure message to the Iranian general.

"P won't move. Does not trust that you will hold back missiles and prompt more nukes."

In less than a minute, a response.

"I will control all forces. P will have best opportunity in history. If he shrinks, we do have a hook to drag him in."

The Director knew what that 'hook' was, and it sobered him. Iran had enough nuclear fuel with Russian tags or markers to make dozens of dirty bombs. In fact, his sources had already told him that they were made and in Syria, ready to deploy in every major Israeli site. He knew the response of the Jews would be a massive nuclear retaliation on his country for which, under the circumstances, they were poorly prepared. The consequences globally were frightening even for him. He cursed the Jews for being so technologically advanced.

Russia's only hope of leading the Dreamworks coalition was the adherence of the Israelis to the new Unity Treaty. They had committed, but UN inspectors were barely on the ground. His sources said there were now nearly a thousand devices to disarm. That would take well over a year to accomplish and validate. That gave him time to maneuver but he had to find a way to persuade P to provide the necessary leadership. He did not want this hot-head in Tehran taking the initiative.

"No need for any hook. Let treaty work. I will handle P."

There was no reply for a few minutes, then, "OK for now."

Seeking confirmation, he then replied to Yehudah, "Are DBs in Syria?"

A few moments later, "Yes, 25. Hz has two."

Now Naryshkin cursed the Iranians.

Brussels

Abdul received, in diplomatic pouch, the instructions from Pope Pietro on using all his media contacts and channels to announce that Mossad was discovered to be responsible for the attack on the previous Pope which had led to his resignation. Pietro would make known this 'fact' to the public in a couple of days and note how thankful he is for the new Unity Treaty which will hopefully make such actions a thing of the past.

Of course, Abdul knew this was coming; he had learned that as with most high-level assassinations or their attempts, the Council was involved. The attack on the former Pope, Pietro had organized personally. It disgusted him as he pondered this impostor and increasingly, he realized the true nature of the people in this Council.

He wanted to somehow get his family to safety and wondered where in all this world that could be. Several messages to them recently had gone unanswered. Ibrahim did not reply either.

He left the EU offices to assure himself of a higher degree of security. Although the President and several high-ranking Parliament officials knew of his role in the Unity Treaty, he personally made sure his name and face were not publicized in association with it. Most people in the West were not familiar with him.

Finding his traditional 'secure' place to work, he ordered a sweet coffee and connected his laptop with the public WiFi. He ran a scan on surrounding devices and then jammed the one signal he found threatening. After this, he sent a file of pre-prepared messages and tactical instructions for the Mossad communique that would be in the news, world-wide, the next day immediately following the Prelate's announcement. By this time, his assets in the major media channels were well coordinated and knew how to spin the story as Abdul, or rather the Council, wanted.

The reports would read, "Mossad out of control. Vatican willing to forgive but insists new treaty must be adhered to for the safety of the world. EU, US, Russia, UN all angry at incident."

With enough creative detail to be convincing, the Israeli government would be incentivized to expedite disarmament. Abdul considered this to be good for the whole Middle East for as yet, he was not read-in to the Dreamworks initiative.

Roma, 30 days later

Pietro wasted no time in furthering his Interreligious Program with the Patriarchs, the Sunnis and the Shi'ites. A month after the explosive Mossad articles, religious unity seemed like the only way to ensure the lasting peace initiated by the Unity Treaty. Impressed with the persuasive power of Abdul's propaganda campaign in the West, the Pope invited him to join the dialog. As he had already done significant work for the Prelate on the topic, it made good sense to the Leader as well.

"Do you think we can bridge the gaps to create a truly United Muslim Union, Abdul?" Pietro asked in the privacy of his papal office.

"Your Holiness, what we need to accomplish that is a leader - one who is a descendant of the Prophet, to satisfy the Shi'ites and at the same time supports the Sunni consensus on leadership as well as the concept of the global caliphate. Essentially, it must be someone broadly acknowledged as the Mahdi."

The Pope mused about that for a couple of minutes and murmured, "That's doable."

Abdul followed with, "Of course the Jews look for their own Messiah, but most declare he will be the one who delivers them from their enemies and allows them to build another temple."

Pietro nodded impatiently, "Yes, yes, that's well understood. Do you have any opinions about the splinter groups?"

"The Orthodox and Evangelicals?" Abdul asked.

"I'm not concerned with the latter. They will die out soon enough. The Patriarchs are another story. They have established strong governmental support in most places..."

"Perhaps, then, they will respond to governmental pressure and conform to your Unity Faith?"

"I thought of that," the Pope boasted. "Until now, we could not make it happen but, as you know, it has become a different world in the last year or so. The imminence of global nuclear catastrophe has changed a lot of minds. Nothing is sacred anymore. Survival of our race dominates all rational thinking. Thus, the Unity Faith will carry that banner above all."

Now the Pontiff smiled, 'I can make that work,' he thought. At the same time, he noted discomfort in Abdul.

"Are you with me? Abdul, you seem distracted or disturbed. Which is it?"

"Neither your Holiness. It just occurred to me who would fit your plans."

"It does seem obvious, doesn't it? Does that bother you?"

"Oh, no... no. I was wondering about the pedigree..."

"Nonsense. You yourself are the master persuader. You will create the proper pedigree for him."

At this, the Pope stood and excused Abdul.

It wasn't long afterward Abdul was summoned to Frascati by Ismail. Along the way he told the driver to pull over. On the side of the road, he puked violently. Finally realizing the implications, the consequences of his work the last three years, he could not stomach it. The whole time, he had thought he was serving his maker, he had always thought Allah would be pleased. However, he now understood that he was serving the darkest power on earth and it tortured him.

Returning to the limo, he told the driver to continue, "Bad food, I think," he said.

At the estate, Ismail was distracted. When Abdul entered his office, he was virtually yelling at someone on the phone to execute the German plan immediately and to be ready for France soon. He wrapped up quickly when he saw the PM enter.

"We are approaching the pinnacle of our plans in Europe, Abdul. You don't need, as yet, to know all the details, but we are building upon your work and using many of your contacts. You should be proud. Now, I cannot entertain you. Too much in the works. I called you here to send you off to Damascus and perhaps Riyadh to join with Baruch, Ashfin, Yehuda and some of their operatives. You need to apply your skills to managing our various partners in Dreamworks. Baruch will fill you in. We have perhaps a year at most to accomplish the entire plan so we will reassign you immediately from the EU to the new embassy in Jerusalem."

"Will the President release me so quickly?"

"Trust me, there will be no problem, none at all."

Abdul left the estate and asked the driver to take him to his hotel. Upon arriving, he made the call he knew he had to make. It was time, and he had no one else to turn to.

"James," it was voicemail, "I have finally realized something, and it is terrifying. I would endanger you if I gave any details. But I need help. I'm wondering if your sister-in-law might have some way of assisting. I'm on my way to Damascus and then Jerusalem. Please call me tomorrow. I'll be in flight the rest of today... And please, my friend, pray for me."

Roma

Abdul knew as much about government stabilizing and destabilizing as any man having lived it for much of his career. He had always wanted Khartoum to be better than it was and over time, he realized that the corruption, greed, hypocrisy and self-interest wasn't limited to his own government. He's studied Marx and Lenin; he'd studied Jefferson and Ghandi. Their writings were all the reflections of the perceived needs of their times but none of them accurately addressed the fundamental need of humankind – a fulfilling connection with the divine.

Of course, their philosophies had birthed revolutions and governments based on or promising a better way, a better life for all. Nevertheless, all of them fell short because none of them exalted this fundamental need. In the end, all of them fell into the same traps over and over again. His talks with James had actually helped him to clear the foggy nonsense of failed humanism.

That said, he was also better equipped to see the weak points in France and Germany that could be most easily leveraged to create a critical destabilization. Germany had masked their fundamental desire for cheap labor to fuel their export economy with fake humanitarian gestures eventually pushing the same upon the whole EU via immigration quotas. The Germans as a whole were simply 'genetically wired' to desire domination – if not militarily, then economically. This was something that could be exploited, he believed.

The French were, as a whole, comfort-seekers. He saw them as driven more by the pursuit of 'human needs' whether for survival or pleasure. Of course, he knew his 'broad-brush' view of both cultures was a gross generalization but served nevertheless as adequate postulates to expose "leverage points" for destabilization.

He himself had no desire to see any government fall. Painful memories of his own experiences still haunted him. However, his own driving passion was to safeguard his loved ones, so he strategized for the Council. He was a hypocrite in this regard and the awareness of it tortured him.

As he took on the work of negotiating the details of the Unity Treaty, he had turned over all his plans to Ismail and was hopeful they would never be used.

Frascati

After receiving Abdul's report months earlier, Ismail was satisfied that he had arranged most of the financial and political logistics involved in overthrowing the governments of Germany and France and could pull the trigger on either within a few weeks. The final target was…

The phone rang and indicated Pietro was calling. He answered.

"I need to speak directly with… "

"Let me see if I can help you first," Ismail interrupted.

"We may have a problem in-house. I'm sensing Mahgoub is getting distracted and he needs to refocus."

"I have noticed that as well, but what makes you think that?"

"Let's just say I have a gift. I can sense it. Has his family been in contact with him?" the Pontiff replied.

"No, they can't. The father-in-law is dead, and his wife is no longer in our 'sanctuary'."

"Is that situation secure? Does he know? And what about his children?"

"Pietro, rest assured, the knowledge of her departure is very secure and no, he is unaware. His children were more problematic. The Leader wants to maintain our leverage, so we're hunting them all down. When we locate them, we'll isolate them separately as well in a secret location."

"In any event, maybe he needs a short message from his wife if you know what I mean."

"Perhaps, but I'm confident that I know what the real problem is. And I will take care of it. Thanks for the call."

Chapter 19

Athens

In twenty-two years of operation, the Food Bank had distributed more than 20,000 tons of food to orphanages, nursing homes and rehab centers. James was a longtime volunteer. His usual walk from home to the facility along Papagou boulevard was uneventful. The traffic was crazy as usual and again he was glad he didn't drive in it. Vanessa was home-schooling Tasha and Michael.

As he neared, he paid little attention to the large van pulling up as it appeared to be from a donor company. However, as he turned for the entrance, the van door opened; immediately, two large men jumped out and grabbed him. In another moment, he was hooded, tied up and the van was speeding off. The other men inside were shouting at each other in Greek and Arabic. Of course, James was scared but oddly calmer than he would have expected.

The captors were apparently unsure of their orders. James spoke Greek but not Arabic. He could tell they wanted to be sure they got paid and didn't trust the people at the airstrip.

'Airstrip?!' he thought. He began immediately to worry about Vanessa and the children. Were they OK? What had he done? Were these people extremists? He'd gotten threats before many times due to sharing his faith. Perhaps this was related.

"Listen, I think you've gotten the wrong person! I'm nobody and I have no money," he said in Greek.

Someone punched him in the gut. Not the worst blow he'd ever received but enough to wind him. He struggled at the hand ties but then someone kicked him in the worst place. His eyes watered and he went neonatal for a while. The pain was excruciating. The rest of the trip he tried to listen to discern where they were headed. 'Which airstrip?' he wondered. The traffic noise disappeared, and the road got rough. In thirty minutes or so, he thought he could smell the ocean.

The van stopped. Soon, he was dragged out and then into a small plane. Again, he heard arguing about payment followed by gunshots. At this point, two people got in the plane with him.

"Where are you taking me!?" he shouted in Greek.

There was no answer. The plane took off and rose rapidly after which the pilot radioed in Italian to someone an estimated arrival time of about two hours.

"Who do you think I am??" James yelled out.

"Shut up!" came the response.

"Keep him quiet," one of the men said to the other.

Immediately, James was duck-taped over his mouth and the hood replaced over his head. While it was off, he saw that it was a small plane, single engine prop four-seater and his captors were both Italian.

Two hours later, the plane landed on a rough airstrip. Promptly, he was hauled off the craft and thrown into a box truck, or so it seemed. With his hands tied securely, he bounced around in the back, banging his head repeatedly. At one point, a large heavy crate fell on him and knocked him out.

When he came to, James was still tied but the hood and tape were gone. Around him was a dark, cold cell with an old wood door and stone walls. He was seated on a metal chair and the only light was what streamed in via the small window in the door.

"Hello! Where am I?!" he cried. His head ached terribly. Straining to listen, he could hear some muffled speaking, again in Arabic, outside the cell, after which the door opened. A sinister looking man with an angry face entered carrying a baton. Without a word he struck James on the side of the head. That was followed quickly by blows to his midsection and thighs. The pain was immediate, sharp and piercing. James cried out loudly.

"What did he tell you?!" the man shouted with a thick Arabic accent.

"Who?! Who do you mean?" James stuttered then closed his eyes, "Lord, please strengthen me," he prayed.

Another blow to his stomach.

"What did Mahgoub tell you?!!" the torturer screamed.

Then, out of nowhere someone else, unseen before, smashed his face with a fist again and again. After that, he was bleeding profusely and had to spit to breathe.

"Noth-nothing. He's just a friend."

"How do you know him?"

"We met in Athens at a cafe years ago. Why?"

Another blow to his head. Now he was so dizzy, he nearly fainted.

"I ask the questions!"

Water was thrown in his face or so he thought. Then he realized he was drowning and someone was holding the back of his head. He struggled violently but to no avail. At the last second, he was jerked upward, barely breathing. His lungs burned like they were going to explode.

"What did he tell you?" Again, his interrogator sneered at him with disgust.

"Abdul is a good man…" he choked out.

"That's not what I'm looking for. I'll give you five minutes to consider my question."

Another middle eastern man entered. "Ismail, there's a call for you."

James faded in and out of consciousness murmuring prayers for strength and help. The five minutes became two hours. Now on the floor, he looked at what appeared to be a new light shining warmly in the room.

"I hear you, James. Do not fear."

He recognized the voice and knew Who it was. And with those words, his heart was strengthened.

A few minutes later, his tormentor reappeared.

"One last time. What did Mahgoub tell you? Did he mention anything about Dreamworks?"

"Dreamworks? No. I tell you he's never spoken about anything like that. I have no idea what you're talking about. I am no threat to you, whoever you are. I'm simply trying to share the love of God."

At that very moment, he saw another man pass by the still open cell door.

"Pope Pietro?!" James was shocked.

The tormentor looked angrily behind him at the Pontiff and then with unbridled force used the large baton to smash James' skull. He picked the body up off the floor slightly and let it fall again.

"Dispose of it!" he yelled.

He glared at the Pope. "I wasn't done!"

Later that day, James' mutilated body was found in a back alley of Rome near via Farnesia with only a card from the Food Bank in his pocket.

Chapter 20

Tel Aviv

Tamar's team was able to stay in front of the antiviral work done by the Iranians and Russians. Their deeply embedded APT code together with the intel their covert agents relayed was enough to continue to tune the persistence factors in the Pan APT virus remotely and enhance its self-mutating appearance. Masked within the broadcast of common cosmic radiation noise, their updates to the virus went undetected and continued to frustrate those trying to clean systems of the malware.

Of course, this tuning work kept everyone busy virtually 24/7 but it was worth it since enemy systems down meant enemies incapacitated. Neither Cyber Defense nor anyone in Mossad could imagine a serious threat being mounted in light of the continued success with Pan and especially under the new Unity Treaty.

Tamar was no different. That is, until she uncovered non-update data streams being piggybacked on her own. It was alarming because no one had authority to compromise the update stream. First, she audited the entire development process but found no clues. Next, she successfully isolated the foreign data in the noise and found that it was not even viral code but rather a series of messages which she had to decrypt and found to be in Hebrew and Farsi.

Actually, it was ingenious, and she would never have noticed save for a single spurious harmonic in the 'noise' that acted as a key. She traced the source to the team's own random noise generation system that was fed in turn to weather satellites as well as into many Iranian network nodes.

IDF IT did the operational maintenance on that system and since she didn't know if she could trust them she backdoored the Tracker application they used to log their maintenance and found that one person had been routinely applying updates to the generators. She was alarmed to find that these updates coincided exactly with her team's Pan updates.

It took her nearly a week to decrypt the first messages which revealed Israeli troop movement, capabilities and assessed vulnerabilities in the North and South. They did not indicate a message source or a destination. This was clearly betrayal of the nation's security, but as yet she had no idea how long it had been going on.

Tamar took her research to her superiors in Cyber, but they decided to turn it over to Mossad since the threat apparently was both internal and foreign. A few days later, she learned the signals she discovered and decrypted were deemed to be simply stochastic and coincidental.

'What?!' she thought. 'There's no way to produce intelligible content with purely random signals! How stupid do they think I am?'

The same evening, she received that feedback, she was visited at home by a man she didn't know. Responding to the doorbell, she found him, grim and with gun in hand.

"May I come in?" he said dryly.

She tried to shut the door, but he forced it open and knocked her to the floor. Closing the door behind him, he turned his back for an instant. That was long enough for Tamar to grab her own gun from under the sofa seat cushion, a precaution Yaakov had suggested. The intruder turned back and raised his gun to fire, but before he could get a round off, Tamar blasted three slugs into his chest. He fell backward against the front door dead.

With her heart racing, she searched the man for an ID but there was none. His gun was a Mossad .22 LRS Beretta, used frequently by the agents. She bagged it and looked for anything else on the corpse. In a coat pocket, there was a picture of her and on the back, her address. Suddenly, she realized that this man would certainly have other associates that would eventually come after her.

She grabbed her phone and dialed the only other person she felt she could trust - Yaakov.

"I think I discovered a covert group of traitors who are informing someone in Iran of our top secret IDF information. There's a dead agent in my front room right now..."

"Tamar! Are you all right?"

"Yes, but I'm scared. I sent my discovery up the chain in Cyber Defense. They brought in a Mossad Director I didn't know. This afternoon, they told me to turn over all my data and that my discovery was only coincidental, part of an ongoing disinformation campaign. What do I do?!"

"Do you have a Go-bag?"

"Yes, somewhere, I forgot where I stored it. I can find it."

"Grab it. Don't worry about the clean-up. Get out of there immediately and meet me at the Cafe Michael on Halamed Hei in Jerusalem. They're open tonight until 10:30 or so. I'll meet you at 10:00 inside. Got it? Inside."

"Yaakov. This is crazy! I've never shot anyone before," she exclaimed.

"I know. But you're not alone. I've encountered others who are finding out frightening things just like you. Now, get out of there right away! Tonight at 10. I'll be there."

Tel Nof IAF base south of Tel Aviv

Col. Yaakov Katz was quick to leave his office in the Rehovot base also known as AFB 8. Nuclear ordinance was stored there so there were several security checks to pass through. He knew he could make the drive to Jerusalem in under an hour, but traffic was unpredictable. He stopped by his quarters to pick up his own Go-bag and firearms. Speeding away, his apprehension was rising rapidly. Something terrible was approaching; at least that's what his gut told him.

The timing of Tamar's call was uncanny. Earlier, he had spoken with Mintz, his co-pilot, and learned that she was being tailed for the last few days. Before this, Baruch had tried to coerce her into telling him what she knew about Katz and the nature of his relationship with Tamar. She was alarmed at the General's apparent intent and said that he should be very careful. Baruch had the reputation of being a butcher to anyone he thought posed a threat - to Israel and to himself.

What Yaakov and Tamar did not know as yet was that the General had already unleashed his wolf.

Jerusalem

As he entered the city, Yaakov turned off 50 and headed down Azza St. making a hard right on Ha Ari. He continued to Shneorson Square where he found parking and continued on foot to the cafe. He arrived well ahead of time and carefully inspected the surrounding area - no cars, no vehicles at all. Only a handful of guests remained inside none of which were tourists.

'As expected,' he thought.

Going inside, he sat and ordered a beer. As he did so, a couple of other guests left. Did they seem hurried? 'All the better,' he surmised. A few minutes later, it was 10:00 and Tamar was nowhere to be seen. He peered out the window at the dimly lit street and wondered if he shouldn't have just picked her up. As he looked for her, another car stopped on the other side of the street. No one exited but the headlights went out. Just then, he saw her walking quickly toward the cafe, glancing over her shoulder a couple of times.

Standing up, he left some shekels on the table and made for the door. As he stepped outside, Tamar saw him and ran the remaining ten meters.

"I'm sure I was followed!" she whispered. The street was dark and quiet, so her voice carried.

"Here, give me your bag," he answered, "let's leave now in my car. It's just down the street."

They turned and power-walked the 100 meters or so to his Porsche Boxster. About two-thirds of the way there, the headlights on the car parked across from the cafe went back on and it began to move in their direction. Their power walk became a run, and in a few seconds, they were in his car racing away. The other vehicle pursued for a few minutes and then suddenly pulled over.

"Let them go," Yehuda told the driver. "I can find them when it suits me."

Yaakov drove the Boxster like he flew a F-35. In a few minutes, they were outside the city.

"Were they chasing us or not?" Tamar asked him.

"It seemed that way," he offered. "Maybe we're just a little on edge, but I'm going to take you to a friend's house. I haven't seen her in a couple of years, but we went through pilot training together. We should be safe there. I don't even know, for sure, that we're in danger, but my pilot senses are telling me we've been painted, and we better take evasive action."

It was well after midnight when they arrived in Beersheba.

Beersheba

Dr. Alina Karchevsky was head of a major research center at Ben Gurion University. Yaakov hadn't seen her for over a year, but they had been close friends. Alina did well in pilot training with IAF but after her service tour, she decided to finish her PhD.

"I hope she hears us," he said in a hushed tone as he knocked and rang.

There was no answer, so he then phoned her. A groggy voice answered.

"Lina, it's Yaakov."

"Hot Shot? It's after 12. What's up?"

"Please let us in."

"Us? Who's with you?"

"A Friend. Come get the door."

"Yaakov, I'm in Tel Aviv. Just look behind the...
"Yes, yes, I remember now." He grabbed the electronic key that opened the door and disarmed the security system. "Thanks, Lina. We'll be out in morning, I promise. Please don't tell anyone we're here. I call you later and explain."

Tamar was worn out from the anxiety. She fell out quickly on the couch. Meanwhile Yaakov sat and stared outside wondering if they were safe. He recalled his intense distrust of Baruch and was increasingly convinced he was somehow a security threat. But how could a senior officer in the IDF be a threat, especially in light of directing the Little Samson mission? Clearly, Tamar had a target on her, and he was certain he did as well. Was there a connection? Was it the mission? Or the General? What had they stumbled upon? His questions went on and on in his mind until he finally fell out.

In the morning, he remembered Lina had a burner phone somewhere and he began searching through her desk. He found the phone and then saw something else - a device the size of a big gyro that was connected to her computer. Curiosity got the best of him; he knew Lina was always inventing something incredible and she often asked his opinion. He booted the computer and the device powered on also. He noticed an executable program on the desktop and double-clicked. A new screen appeared that seemed to show a simple drawing of the room. A dialog box opened with the words, "Identify target." Yaakov studied it for a few seconds, then picked up the stylus next to the screen and drew a circle on the touch-screen around the couch where Tamar lay sleeping.

The program dialog changed to, "Please confirm target."

Yaakov chuckled, 'This ought to be good.'

He circled the couch again and the dialog box disappeared and the circle glowed green. Nothing seemed to happen for a few seconds but as he started to get up, to his amazement, the couch with Tamar on it vanished.

He gasped and ran over to where it had been and stumbled to the floor tripping over Tamar's outstretched leg. Tamar then stood up and appeared or at least part of her appeared. Still tired, she ambled to the bathroom and as she got a couple of feet away from the couch, she was entirely visible.

Yaakov could feel the cushions, the sofa was indeed still there, but standing back from it, it was completely gone, invisible.

"Wow!" he shouted. He approached the couch again and sat on it. As he did so, it came in sight along with the rest of the room. Standing and then looking at it below, it was gone as was his abdomen and legs.

"This is amazing!"

He went back to the desk and clicked on the tab that seemed to indicate "Undo". Again, nothing seemed to happen for a few seconds, then the sofa reappeared. Thinking this would be a lifesaver, he found a thumb drive in the desk drawer and copied the executable program to it.

He also found what appeared to be a setup file labeled 'Hide and Seek' and documentation with the same name indicating it was new and experimental. When it was all copied, he shut down the computer and disconnected the attached device.

He scribbled a note: "Lina, please forgive me. I'll return it ASAP."

Tamar burst from the bathroom, phone in hand, clearly in shock. "James is dead!! I have to see my sister!"

"Who is James?" Yaakov asked as tenderly as he could.

"My brother-in-law. I just got a text from Nessa, my sister. She's stunned with grief. The police found his mutilated body in a back alley of Rome, but they aren't even going to investigate, and she doesn't know why."

At this point, she couldn't hold back and began weeping profusely. She sat next to Yaakov on the sofa and grabbed his hand.

"Can you pray with me?" she asked.

He was startled, but then said, "Sure."

"Expecting a Jewish recitation like he remembered from his youth, he was surprised when she said, "Lord, please help my sister and protect her and Tasha and Michael. She taught me to trust in you. Amen."

"Tamar, something bigger than we suspect is going on. I'm being followed, you're being followed, we both believe Baruch is dirty and now one of your relatives is dead," Yaakov said gently.

"What should we do??" she asked, wiping her eyes.

"I'm not sure, but you did just pray, that's something I know nothing about. Probably wouldn't hurt to ask Him for guidance. I'm going to go out and get us some supplies. Just hang out here and don't make any calls. Our phones may have already been traced. I'll make it quick. I found a burner that Lina had. When I get back, you can call your sister on it."

Beersheba

There was a market nearby where Yaakov bought food. He returned and placed it his car. He also destroyed his old phone and tossed the remains away. The car was safe - he had removed the tracking chip long ago as a security precaution. Before going inside the house, he sat in the driver's seat and used the burner to call his work. His aide answered.

"Col. Katz' office. Chief Mier speaking."

"Chief, I'm taking some emergency leave for the next two days."

"Sir, do you know Mossad has been here asking for you. They grilled each of the squadron commanders and hammered on me as well. Seems very odd. Are you OK? Can I get you anything?"

"Just file my leave papers, Chief. I'll clear it later with the General. And... just act normal. If anyone asks, I'm getting some R&R in Eliat."

"Understood, Sir."

He ended the call quickly. The next number he called was Lina's. He wanted to tell her about borrowing the new tech. A strange voice answered, "Yes," there was a long pause.

"Who is this?" Yaakov asked.

"Who is this??"

"I'm calling for Dr. Karchevsky. Did I get the wrong number?"

"This is Detective Eisen with the Israel Police, Tel Aviv District. What is your relationship with Dr. Karchevsky?"

"She is a long-time friend. Why? What's going on? Let me speak to her."

"Give me your name."

He ended the call. Next, he called her office in Beersheba.

"Hello, I'm calling for Alina. I tried to reach her in Tel Aviv but,..." he started.

"She's dead!" her assistant cried. "Is this Col. Katz?"

"Yes. Are you sure?! I just spoke with her last night."

"The police said she was shot early this morning. I can't believe it. She was such a good person. Why would anyone want to hurt her?" There was a pause. "She left me a message to make sure you had everything you needed. She said you were at her place."

"I'm fine. Have you told anyone else about her message?"

"No."

"Good. For now, please don't."

"Excuse me," she answered, "someone just came in. Can I help you?"

The line went dead.

Beersheba

He got out of his car and headed for the entrance to Lina's home when he heard sirens approaching. Running to the door, he opened it and shouted, we need to leave… now! Tamar, come on!"

She jumped up and ran out to where he was waiting, then they both rushed to his car. Tamar got in, but before Yaakov could do the same, two men jumped him from behind. His combat survival training kicked in and he decked one of the assailants who stayed on the ground. The other started to pull out a gun and would have shot but he got a large rock to the back of the head and fell. With the body on the ground before her Tamar smiled but looked scared at the same time.

Yaakov heard the sirens getting closer but took the time to grab the muggers' guns and IDs then both of them jumped into the Porsche and sped out of Beersheba east on 25 and then south on 40.

"Are we headed south?" Tamar asked.

"Yes." His mind was spinning, wondering what was happening.

"Good. That's the direction I got. Actually, that's all I got."

"What do you mean?" he asked her, one eye on the road.

"When I prayed. I asked for guidance. In my mind, it seemed like He said to go south."

Yaakov didn't answer but thought if there was a God, this was good time to listen.

About two and a half hours later, they stopped outside Eliat. Along the way, they had not talked much. Tamar thought of her sister and Yaakov about his old friend Lina.

"So, you believe you're hearing from... God?" he finally asked.

"Yes, but if you had asked me that a year ago, I'd have laughed at you."

"OK, so what changed? I mean you're a scientist and probably the best data person in the country."

"Do you really want to know or are you wanting to make fun of me?"

His face was serious, "Tamar, I think you know how I feel about you. I would not tease you on this. But here we are on the run from people who will stop at nothing to get to us. If you have something to share, please do so. I want to know how this works and if it's real."

She did what she could to explain, but she felt like it was inadequate. After all, it wasn't just Vanessa's words that convinced her to believe. Yaakov seemed sincere and listened carefully. Afterward, he simply said, "OK, where to now?"

"Aqaba, then North."

Her voice shook a little. This was crazy for her too. He looked at her and smiled, feigning bravado, but she could see love as well as apprehension in his eyes. Before long, they had crossed the border into Jordan and were all the way to Wadi Musa.

"Take the device with us," she told Yaakov as the vehicle stopped.

"What in the world are we doing here? Isn't this just a tourist site?" he replied.

Just then a couple of young boys came to the car and offered to be guides. Tamar said yes before Yaakov could answer and soon, they were winding their way past ruins and through a deep narrow canyon. Before long, it began to get dark. The boys tugged at Yaakov seeking payment.

After getting some money from him, they ran off back through the canyon. Meanwhile, the two desperate Israelis found shelter in a cave. The ensuing night was cold, and they wrapped each other up in the blankets they'd brought, holding each other for warmth. The danger of Beersheba and Tel Aviv now seemed a world away.

Wadi Musa

Over the next few days, Tamar and Yaakov explored the ancient ruins they found. As they ventured further and further from the canyon entrance, they found themselves entirely alone. For quite some time, Tamar led the way deeper and deeper into the hills far beyond any and all tourist sites.

"Yaakov, come quick! Look at this!" she finally exclaimed.

He ran to where she stood pointing at a large carved entrance into the mountainside with steps leading up to it. They both climbed up and went inside. That's when Yaakov took a deep breath and stared in disbelief.

"Who could have done this?!" he said.

Both of them sensed a supernatural power at work. Yaakov wondered if the Jordanian government had created what they witnessed. It was immense, expansive and fully equipped with generators. Chamber after chamber after chamber was filled with supplies. He had to catch his breath. Taking Tamar by the hand, he led her back outside and they sat down. Yaakov looked at her with utter amazement.

"It's like Dimona but even better. Did you know this was here? Do you know who made this place?" he asked, virtually in shock.

"No. But it must be for a purpose. You saw. I just asked Him, and we went where He said to go. I'm as surprised as you."

They sat there in the sun, pondering what being led to this seemingly supernaturally provided and constructed facility could mean. After several minutes, Yaakov asked, "Tamar, can you tell me more? Can you help me understand more about this faith of yours?"

She looked deep in his eyes and saw that he was sincere.

"Yes, of course."

The next day, they began to explore. From the control center, Yaakov and Tamar could run the facilities of the entire refuge – lights, environmentals, power consumption, alarm conditions and communications, both internal and external. They searched everywhere and found no markings, no company logos, no serial numbers – nothing to indicate the origin of the equipment.

They roamed through the vast maze of lighted arched passageways, 13 feet high and reinforced with steel and concrete and were impressed that the lights turned on and off with them as they moved. One day, Yaakov traveled almost twelve kilometers in one direction through them. There was some signage – in Hebrew and English. Eventually, they estimated that the refuge covered as much as 28 square kilometers and contained heavy equipment for expansion.

Enormous water tanks in the water treatment plant provided water and water pressure to the whole place being filled by aquifers over 1000 meters deep which were later estimated by engineers to contain more fresh water than the Mountain Aquifer and was completely unknown. Salinity levels were less than 50 mg/l and thus quite potable. Amazingly efficient water pumps could run on fuel or power cells charged by the exterior solar arrays.

Close by was a series of seriously equipped engine rooms for supplying additional power for lights and equipment, ventilation and other environmental controls, and was highly regulated eliminating virtually all power spikes and dropouts. Each room housed half a dozen large engines and associated equipment. There were also three vast rooms filled with solar conversion and integration equipment including innumerable arrays of batteries. Engineers later found that power was supplied as DC, 50 Hertz AC and an entirely different type of conductible power based upon amplified gravitational waves.

Behind the area with this heavy equipment they stumbled upon an incredibly vast chamber that appeared to be a warehouse containing hordes of supplies for further construction and expansion. Connected to it were several large chambers designed for vehicle storage and maintenance containing hundreds of electric vehicles.

Continuing on, they discovered numerous large completely equipped kitchens which together could quite adequately feed many thousands of people. Close by, were various size dining halls, again completely equipped.

What amazed Tamar were the fully functional hospital wards and medical units. She had no idea what some of the equipment was for until she read the provided manuals. Again, no indication of who or where they were made.

In another direction were dozens and dozens of passageways with connected living quarters, all furnished modestly. As you approached the control room, there were numerous meeting chambers and amazingly, a grand garden chamber or rather network of chambers all illuminated with artificial sunlight.

Chapter 21

Frascati

"The Leader will not tolerate this failure. I hope for your sake that you will tie up those loose ends quickly." Ismail lectured Yehuda who was embarrassed that he and his team had not eliminated the security risk which Yaakov and Tamar presented.

"It is being handled." Yehuda growled.

"I've had my hands full in Europe. Now that the treaty is established, you and Baruch have to handle Dreamworks." Ismail said.

"I can read Mahgoub in to it now, right?"

"No, not yet. Maybe not at all. I had to deal with one of his own 'loose ends' recently, and I'm going to see how he reacts to that. Pietro has sensed that something is off with him as well, but we've invested too much in him to make a quick decision. I'll let you know."

He sent a secure message to the Leader about Abdul and that he was going to meet with him in Jerusalem. The reply read, "I have a backup ready if needed. Your call. Use utmost discretion. We do not want to lose his connections. Return ASAP. I'm ready to initiate on Germany. Want you in place."

"Hmm, maybe a quick decision is in order after all," he said to himself.

Jerusalem

Abdul paced the room with a growing sense of panic. He had tried to contact Aliya many times with no reply and now Ibrahim was unresponsive. He thought of just getting on a plane to Khartoum, but he knew he would only endanger her more. In addition, he felt like Aziz was dead and the worst of it was that he couldn't contact James or Vanessa.

His world was toppling in on him and he was convinced that it was because of his own doing, his vanity and unspoken desire for importance and notoriety. He now feared for not only his family and friends, but for the whole world. It didn't take a crystal ball to see what the Council had in mind for the Middle East, for the EU and for Israel. He had worked in the midst or on the periphery of it all, and it was pure evil - a coming reign of terror.

And he had been so stupid as to think that he was 'making a difference', doing the right thing in the name of his faith. What faith?? He had used deception and justified it for the cause. Now, the truth of his actions and the depravity of his true motives seemed to stare at him and sneer like the face of Aziz or the face of Pietro.

He tried calling James again and the line went to voicemail. He had no other number for Vanessa but then he recalled that her sister, Tamar had given him a card with her contact info. He searched his briefcase and then his wallet and finally found it tucked away and now somewhat faded. Checking his phone, he realized it was only 5:30 AM so he decided to call later that morning. Ismail wanted to meet mid-morning and he had an ominous feeling about it. He even double-checked his gun, a 9mm but a decent deterrent if needed, he thought.

'Has it come to this? Are we all just pawns in a huge master-game?'

Suddenly, his fear turned to anger and then rage. Then, after ranting at the sky, at Allah, at Aziz, he felt utterly condemned. Where was truth? Where was comfort?

His phone rang.

'Too early for Ismail,' he thought as he answered. There was no number.

"Mr. Mahgoub? Abdul?" a female voice asked.

"Yes, who is this?"

"Abdul, this is Tamar, Nessa's sister. I'm so sorry to bother you so early this morning and you are going to think I'm crazy, but I'll tell you anyway," she began. Then she seemed to speak to someone else, "No, Yaakov, it's important. Abdul, I had a dream last night that got me thinking about you and I realized you may not know about James."

"What about him? I've been trying to reach him."

"Well, I'm sorry to say I have some very sad news to tell you. James was found brutally murdered in Rome. Nessa told me about a week ago but then texted me yesterday that she wanted you to know and she did not have your number."

Abdul was silent. They say you don't really feel shock, but at that moment, he felt it. James had become his dearest friend. He clenched his fist.

"Do the police know what happened? Is Vanessa needing help? Tasha? Michael?"

"Nessa and the children are coping. She was in tears when we talked but she reminded me that she knew he was in peace and that she would see him again. Tasha and Michael don't really understand. I know you were close to them."

"Closer than you can imagine. Tamar, thank you so much. Are you OK?"

"Me? Well actually we, my friend and I, are in some trouble also. We think that we stumbled upon some information that was supposed to stay hidden and now a General in the IDF has someone hunting for us. We had to leave Tel Aviv quickly..."

"A General? An IDF General? Who is it?"

"You probably don't know him though he is very powerful. His name is Baruch."

Abdul nearly dropped the phone.

"Do you think there is any connection with James?" she continued.

"With James?? No...... I don't think so. Never mind. Are you OK? Do you need anything?"

"Abdul, I'll reach out to you again very soon. I'm using a burner phone."

The line went dead.

Jerusalem

Ismail picked an out of the way location - nevertheless, a cafe whose clientele were rumored to be among the powerful of the Israeli politics. It was widely known that Abdul was instrumental behind the scenes in bringing Israel and the Muslim Unity nations together. If he had to 'retire' the former PM, in this location it could be spun as an extremist reaction from either side.

Discretely, he placed the magnetic explosive on the underside of the table. It would be triggered by his phone. It was a method he had used many times before to eliminate those who posed a threat to the Council. Collateral damage was meaningless to him.

Abdul approached the cafe cautiously. He kept thinking of what had happened to James and wondered how he had faced his end. James had been a kind man whereas these people were butchers. A big part of him wanted to retaliate, he knew that somehow the Council was to blame. Undoubtedly, he had died for his faith and his kindness. Abdul shook his head in sadness. How would he himself die? He no longer looked to his own tepid beliefs for support. They had misguided him to cower before these vile men. Considering how he had been used made him tremble with rage. In his pocket was his gun. Would he use it? He didn't want to, but then he did.

As he entered the cafe, Ismail motioned to him to sit down. The morning traffic of clientele was busy. Abdul waved at a couple of people he knew and sat down.

"Hello, my friend. It's good to see you. I see you have gotten acquainted with some of the locals already. Do you have everything you need?"

"The accommodations are fine, and the staff is helpful, Ismail," he replied.

"Good. And by the way, I have something for you. Ibrahim gave it to me for you."

He pulled a photo from his pocket and placed it on the table before Abdul. It was picture of his wife but one he recognized as being at least three years old.

'Bad play, puppeteer,' he thought. Nevertheless, he did not play his hand.

"Why thank you. How kind of you to think of it. I haven't heard from her in almost a month."

"Really? I will make sure Ibrahim is more diligent."

Ismail knew Aliya and her children had escaped their 'house-arrest' and that every message Abdul had received from them over the past few years was phony. Aziz would not give up anything on them which had led to his death and as yet they were in the wind. At that point, he noted anger in Abdul's countenance. It was suppressed but he couldn't hide it completely.

"You know, we received a note of compassionate concern from Pietro about you. He said that you seem to be distracted…"

Abdul could not restrain himself any longer.

"Did you murder my friend?"

Ismail feigned surprise. Abdul was no fool.

"Abdul, my friend, he was clearly leading you into folly and wretchedness. We asked him to back off nicely, but he lashed out at us irrationally. Indeed, it was unfortunate, but we had no choice but to defend ourselves. He was extremely violent. Hopefully, you will now be better able to focus on your work and then rejoin your family."

"Have you killed my family too?"

"Of course not. They are being treated very well."

Suddenly, Ismail excused himself to take a call. "Hang on, Abdul. I'll be right back. I'm sure we can work this out." He left the cafe.

Immediately, Abdul, filled with so much rage, needed to puke so he got up and went to the restroom and found the ceramic throne. Seconds later, a violent explosion knocked him to the floor and part of the restroom's wall caved in on him. Fire, smoke, blood and screams were everywhere. His head and shoulder were wounded and bleeding though not profusely. Shaking loose from the debris, he carefully got to his feet and steadied himself. He could see through the smoke that the cafe was gutted and then sirens began to sound.

He knew this was Ismail's doing and his survival sense told him that if he was going to make it another day alive, he had to stay 'dead'. Stripping his now tattered jacket, he buried it along with one of his IDs in the rubble and made as quick an exit as possible hiding among the wounded and aid workers.

Jerusalem

With the deafening blast still ringing in his ears, Abdul struggled to think clearly. He wandered for what seemed like hours. Finally finding himself on HaUman St., he entered a three-story cement building. He was weary from walking and thought he should call for a ride. But where would he go. The business he had entered evidently sold restaurant supplies. As he fumbled for his phone, he realized it could be tracked and so promptly dumped it in a trash bin. Starting back out the door, he bumped into a tall man, who looked at him carefully.

"I'm sorry. I think I recognize you from briefings I've had on the Unity Treaty. Aren't you Prime Minister Mahgoub?"

The stranger's clothing was a bit worn and a bit soiled, but he seemed strong and alert. His question surprised Abdul.

"Uh… well," Abdul looked around, "yes. I am," he said softly. "What briefings are you talking about?"

"Sir, I still shouldn't talk about that; probably shouldn't have mentioned them. But this is so uncanny, like a divine encounter. My girlfriend mentioned that her sister knew you, but you probably wouldn't recognize her name."

Ever the diplomat, Abdul politely answered, "OK, try me. What's your name and hers?"

"My name is Katz. Col Yaakov Katz."

Abdul's eyes got big. "Fordow?" he whispered.

"Yes, sir. And my girlfriend's sister's name is Vanessa…"

"Vanessa?!" This was no whisper.

"I've been trying to contact her! Then your girlfriend must be Tamar?"

Katz was shocked. He looked around like he felt someone was watching.

"That's right, sir. But what are you doing here?"

"That's a long, long story Colonel."

"Please, call me Yaakov."

"Yaakov, I could ask you the same thing. Where are you stationed? Or are you on leave?"

Yaakov opened the front door of the business and they both went outside.

"Prime Minister…"

"Now you must call me Abdul."

"Abdul, sir, Tamar and I are in a bit of trouble. If you know my name, then you are probably aware of his too. The General who commanded the Fordow mission is… well, it's complicated. But in any event, he seems to be out to get rid of both of us. We were able to get away from his agents a few weeks ago and we're are setting up supply lines."

"Yes, I know this General. And I know how he is connected. In fact, up until today, I was stupid enough to be working with him. But, now tell me, and don't worry because I am on the run as well from these same associates. Why a supply line?"

"Sir, I don't think I should say any more just yet. Let me finish my business inside and we can join up with Tamar. She truly has a connection with," he pointed up, "that I'm only just now learning about."

Abdul smiled and remembered how Tamar had shared with him the same faith as her sister.

"Of course," he replied.

Jerusalem

Yaakov spent almost a half hour with the business owner after which they hugged, shook hands, and hugged again. Then he took Abdul to his car and both of them sped off to another warehouse where they found Tamar waiting. She likewise was discussing something important with the owner who kissed her on both cheeks. When she saw them, she ran to greet Yaakov and to his delight, Abdul.

"God is surely at work!" she said. "Shamir has agreed to help us."

"As did Ruben," he replied. "Tamar, Abdul knows Baruch. I don't know yet how you get this divine guidance, but each turn we take seems more and more amazing. Like I told you on the phone, there he was at Ruben's place when I got there."

"But I am no longer in a position to help you with the General. I wish I could, but I have narrowly escaped an assassination attempt today myself."

"Abdul, we also are in grave danger just being here today," Tamar said. "However, in the last few weeks our lives have drastically changed. There's so much to share, I don't know where to begin. Anyway, we believe God is directing us in what we're doing. And we are utterly amazed at the number of people we are encountering who are suddenly experiencing similar changes and desires to help in our project. Both Jews and Arabs."

Abdul agreed to go with them to other businesses both in Jerusalem and in Beersheba. Along the way, they confided that they had found an amazing facility constructed deep within the side of a mountain with power from generators and solar cells, fresh water from deep underground, and a vast array of living quarters for at least tens of thousands. It was vacant with no indication as to who built it and with the help of Lina's notes, they had set up a cloaking shield that masked the entrances perfectly.

"Many have joined us already," Tamar said. "It's a place of refuge from the coming storm. Not everyone sees it approaching, but it is, and we need to be ready to help those trying to escape."

"I'm not sure I understand. Surely, peace is on the horizon," Abdul answered.

"Tamar found out by digging deep into Baruch files that he has covertly been working with high level people in Iran, Iraq and Russia. We don't know yet all that's going on, but the coming peace is not what it seems to be," added Yaakov.

Abdul for the first time began waking up to this same realization. "I should have known! I've been such a fool. Can I help?" he asked.

The Refuge

Unlike anything he had imagined, the facility was modern, superbly constructed and aptly called the Refuge. Every utility was in place. All that was needed was a working supply line that could keep it stocked with food and medicines as needed. Entrances on the East side and West side of the mountain provided access. Yaakov discovered that they could set up large arrays of additional solar cells and effectively cloak them without inhibiting the solar power generation. Abdul helped him with that work and in the process met dozens of wonderfully loving people all of whom shared in the labor. Each day more people arrived.

The immigrants, if you would, began to arrive as Yaakov and Tamar invited their old friends and trustworthy associates. They also told their supply line contacts to introduce potential refugees and learned how to effectively screen out Council allied people. Abdul was particularly helpful in this.

Surprising to both of them was how many of the arrivals were Messianic Jews. The large majority, of course, were not, but all had very specific reasons for coming. Most sensed a 'calling' or extraordinary circumstances that guided them. About a third of them were married and some of them had children.

There were skilled and unskilled, professionals, shopkeepers, military and civilian, people from all walks of life and generally, except for the children, ranging from 30 to 50 years of age. Abdul helped document the various skills - scientists, engineers, physicians, cooks, technicians, teachers, rabbis, air, land and sea-based military, a few government personnel and tradespeople of all sorts. Except for the few rabbis, the greatest part of them were not religious but all anticipated something catastrophic on the horizon and as a result, all were inclined to pray for help and open to listening to Yaakov share about his new faith.

Tamar kept busy with background checks, not to find the 'cream of the crop' but rather to cross-reference them against names of known Council members and assets that Abdul was able to provide. They knew that the Council had become aware of the refuge and had assigned agents to infiltrate, posing as refugees. All the screening was done at various and randomly changing locations in southern Israel.

Nearly all the attempted infiltrations were stymied by Tamar's background research, but a few had cleansed their data and would have been accepted if it were not for Abdul who recognized them as associates of Yehuda or Baruch. And everyone accepted that for the sake secrecy and security, no personal communications were allowed from the refuge unless screened by Tamar or her 'right hand' Ruben.

The refugees eventually chose leaders and met regularly with Tamar and Yaakov to plan and organize all their activities. Soon, as the numbers began to swell, they volunteered their talents and skills to manage the day to day needs and to activate or enlarge the facility.

But Abdul became the center of attention simply because of his friendliness, his sincerity and his desire to help. Many came to him for guidance and many, just to meet a famous man. Many wanted his view on what was happening in Israel and in the Middle East. One young man who had immigrated to Israel recently from Italy was unique. He wanted specifically to speak with Abdul and asked Yaakov for him by name.

"Mr. Prime Minister..." he started as they sat together.

"My friend, you may call me Abdul," he interjected.

"And I am Ivan. I am a Russian Jew."

"Oh, Yaakov told me you came to Israel from Italy."

"I did. But I came here partly because I... well, let me tell you a story. I went to Italy from Moscow, looking for work. Since I spent time in the Russian Army, I secured a job as a temporary security agent. So anyway, one day we got this assignment that required me to sign a lot of paperwork. It was to guard a prisoner. But I was surprised to learn it was in the lower levels of the Vatican of all places. Everyone there had tight lips, so I knew it was something very secret. The prisoner was questioned about you, Abdul, repeatedly. I couldn't hear much but I heard him say over and over, "He's a good man." So, I guess that wasn't good enough because they beat him terribly. After they left, I couldn't help myself. I had to see who was getting so much of a torture in the Vatican. I snuck into the room and he was on the floor with his hands and feet tied. He was conscious and asked me for a drink. I gave him some water and then he said to please find you, sir, and relay something to you. I thought it would be warning but he said to remember that Christ gave his life to save everyone including you. At first that rubbed me the wrong way, you know, being a Jew. But after I left, I thought I needed to honor his last request. See, just a few minutes later, he was beaten to death and they told us to dump his body in a back alley off Via Farnisia. I felt terrible I couldn't help him but, sir, his dying thoughts were about you."

Abdul started weeping profusely. He knew it had to have been James. The rest of the day he was shaken to the core.

That evening, as Abdul rested, he fell into a deep sleep. As he dreamed, he was approached by a man in brilliant white. The man showed him His hands; they each had a hole. "Who are you?" he said to the man. "You know who I am, and you know I am the truth. I have preserved you for this hour so that you can know my peace and share my life." Then the man touched him, and Abdul's heart leapt. Instantly, he knew all that James had told him was true. He couldn't explain it, but it was true!

When he arose that morning, he found Yaakov and old him all about it and then Tamar. He felt like a child and for the first time in his life, he felt whole.

Abdul began to read the scriptures he once distrusted with an absolute determination to understand them. The enormous weight of guilt he had carried for so many years was gone. For the first time, he looked to the future soberly but with hope and above all, he realized God loved him, just as James had said so many times.

He also came to understand that unlike those harsh eyes of Aziz he once found condemning, God's eyes were filled with grace toward him and that his failures did not define him and no longer controlled him.

"Tamar, I must tell Vanessa. It will encourage her," he excitedly relayed.

"Abdul, we will be going to Beersheba tomorrow for more panels. When we are there you can buy a burner phone and call her," she answered.

Yaakov gave him a hug, "So we're in this now together, huh?" and his face lit up.

"I must tell Aliya and the children. They have to know," he said.

Knowing Abdul had no idea where they were, Yaakov looked at his new brother and answered, "I'll help you find them, Abdul."

Jerusalem

"Simon can only hold the supplies for 24 hours. And we need to find another warehouse to supplement his. The increasing number of cases of staples he is storing for us is drawing attention from his employees. They have been asking where all the food is going and why they aren't loading it," Yaakov shared with Tamar as they arrived in their truck in the industrial district on Ha'uman at Harechev.

"You're right. And he also got a heads-up from the government that he may have to get a tattoo on his hand for a broad commercial-systems test of some kind. That sounds weird to me, but he's ready to join us at the refuge anyway," Tamar responded.

The logistics were complex to be sure, but they always seemed to get 'directed' to solutions when they needed them. And as they pursued together this near-consuming task of managing a refuge for those escaping the coming storm, they discovered a deeper mutual faith and a deepening love for each other.

Yaakov turned to Tamar as they came to a stop and brushed a lock of her hair to the side. She looked at him with eyes so tender, he almost kissed her. Just then, Simon ran out of the building waving his arms and shouting for them to leave immediately. With military reflexes, Yaakov backed up and swung the rig around quickly. Driving away, he saw in the rearview mirror a group of men in black surround Simon and take him to the ground.

"We need to ditch this truck. If that was Mossad, they will track it down," he said angrily.

"Look, that yard with the loading docks over there." Tamar pointed to the left.

Yaakov turned in and brought the rig to a halt next to others that were queued for loading. They jumped out, thankful that their truck was still empty.

"Thank the Lord, Simon warned us in time. Do you think he will be alright?" she asked.

"I think so. He's not guilty of anything except trying to help us. It's us they want and so far, they don't even have any charges I know of," he responded.

"Yes, but we both know they don't need any charges. If they catch us, we're dead."

"I'll use some contacts I have to try to protect him. Anyway, let's get to our safe house and regroup with the other procurement team." Yaakov counted Simon as a good friend.

The safe house was about a kilometer away. As they walked, they kept an eye out just to be sure they weren't being followed. About half way there, Yaakov grabbed Tamar by the arm and pulled her aside into an empty alleyway. He scanned the area, making sure they were alone.

"Tamar, this is pretty nuts. We're trying to do this impossible task with people we don't know trying to hunt us down and yet..." he looked deep into her eyes, "I'm falling so hard for you. Tamar, I love you."

She smiled and grabbed his face in both hands. "Yaakov, you are and always will be a hot shot pilot. You're never afraid to take a chance, even with me... and I love you too," she said with just a hint of jest. She kissed him, really kissed him and in that empty alley, on the run, they realized that they were truly meant for each other. Even in the midst of danger, they had the courage to commit completely to each other, to strengthen each other and to build each other's faith.

Chapter 22

Cairo

Abdul's tragic death hung over the conference in which he was honored for his tireless work to bring about the Unity Treaty. This final conference of more than fifty nations was gathered largely because of his visionary and compelling interactions with their leaders.

On the coattails of the Treaty, this expansive group convening in Cairo used its momentum to finalize the new Atlantic/Mediterranean Union, AMU, which included the EU and Muslim Unity countries as well as the US. Notably absent were Iran, Turkey, Syria, Libya, and Sudan, though the latter two were in a pending status. Even Israel was included.

The many years of negotiation between the EU and US known as the TTIP had finally came to fruition two months earlier so that the combined AMU free trade block represented over seventy-five percent of the world's GDP. As such, the new Union would dominate the world economy and basically dictate its own terms.

By executive order of the interim and soon to be permanent AMU President, NATO would be renamed AMTO and grow to include all members thus representing an overwhelming military capability and the first real assurance of world peace since the PAX Romana.

Russia remained on the sidelines trying to build its own Eurasian Economic Union and appearing conspicuously quiet. China, India and most of the rest of eastern Asia were also busy building their own economic and military confederation. However, neither could compete with the new AMU and they knew it.

Though symbolically signing the Union Agreement in sight of the Pyramids, the members had agreed that the permanent AMU headquarters was to be in Rome and that Leadership would rotate each seven years.

Cairo, in a secure chamber

"Are you absolutely sure he's dead?"

"Sir, there were dozens of casualties, some were even vaporized. But we did find his blood, some clothing and an ID in the debris. There are likely no body parts to be found. The explosive I used was a furnace device specifically for elimination of evidence," answered Ismail.

It was difficult to get any of the Leader's time as dozens of heads of state were in queue to see and congratulate him for his rescue of the German, French and British economies and to thank him for taking the reins of the new AMU which he would accept in a speech that evening.

"Mahgoub is being honored as a hero of the AMU tonight. The last thing we need is for him to reappear and point the finger at you. Do you understand the consequences?"

"Mahgoub is dead, sir. I will make doubly sure of it."

Later that night, the Cairo International Convention Center was a hub of security and activity as thousands from countries all over the world converged to celebrate the dawn of a radically new world. The massive auditorium was packed with dignitaries and media. The mood was electric as speaker after speaker highlighted the work it took to come to this grand occasion along with the promise of prosperity and peace. The last preliminary orator was Pope Pietro himself who took the stage along with Dr. Ibrahim bin Abdul-Kareem Al-Issa.

As they approached the podium, the stage lights dimmed, dramatic music played and the screen behind them began to show pictures of Abdul - in the UN, in Brussels, in nearly every Muslim capital, greeting heads of state and finally arm in arm with the Leader. The music reached a crescendo with the final slide showing the new crest of the AMU.

With the lights still dimmed, a spotlight now shown on Pietro and Ibrahim.

"We must not forget that with each advancement of peace, there is sacrifice. Prime Minister Abdul Mahgoub will be remembered for his dedication to this Union and his final words. I quote, 'Unity is above all. There is no power higher than our own when we are indeed united.'" Pietro stepped aside.

Ibrahim continued, "My friend and college, Abdul was recognized by all of us as the catalyst and master negotiator of the Treaty - moving us all to come together, to put our differences aside and to destroy our weapons of mass destruction. He will be greatly missed."

Both speakers continued with honorariums for several minutes more; then came the final introduction. The Prime Minister of Israel came to the podium and said, "Distinguished guests, it is my honor to introduce the man you have chosen to step in and lead this new Union and guide us to our highest potential."

At this, the crowd rose to their feet and the roar of applause drowned out the speaker who simply backed to the side and with a sweeping hand gesture made way for the Leader. The crowd went wild.

In only a few months, the Leader, at first chosen on an interim basis, but after Cairo, the permanent President, had quickly established control of the new AMTO military as Commander in Chief. Shortly afterward, his directive was that all AMU nations were to contribute ten percent of their GDP to support it. This, along with individual national defense expenditures enabled military technology to soar with unimagined capabilities under his command.

As President of the AMU, he disbanded the EU Presidency but kept the Parliament. He also formed hundreds of inspection teams to police nuclear disarmament throughout the Middle East and in particular, Israel. The new Union indeed became the most powerful force worldwide, dwarfing everything else.

His ten Council members were appointed as AMU ministers and Ismail as Chief of Staff as well.

Chapter 23

Bonn

In the early morning, just before dawn, the team of assassins infiltrated the area surrounding the residence of German Chancellor Angella Steiner. They neutralized and replaced both security guards efficiently as well as the three secret snipers that were on overlook; all the while maintaining security codes and check ins with the BKA.

Shortly afterward, her twelve body guards arrived on schedule in four vehicles to escort her to the Capital. As she exited the building there in central Bonn, the new 'security guards' turned and fired multiple rounds. She was killed instantly. At the same time, shoulder launched missiles fired from the former sniper positions destroyed her convoy completely. It was 6:30 AM. Smoke, debris and emergency vehicles filled the street with German efficiency.

Ismail brought the news to the Leader. "It is done. Steiner is dead," he said, referring to the very outspoken Chancellor.

"Was the evidence left as planned. I want the focus to be on Turkey."

"Yes, sir. Of course, Erdogan will deny it vehemently, but the 'background' will be damning all the way back to Ankara."

"Good. I will announce their temporary severance from the Union pending a thorough investigation while our assets there and in Russia facilitate a gradual welcome 'into the fold' initiative for them from our friends in Moscow. They will have no choice but to go that direction if they want to survive economically."

"It was foolish of Steiner to be so stubborn in opposing your military plans," Ismail replied.

"Ismail, as you know her elimination is not simply a reaction to that opposition. I planned a long while ago to consolidate AMU authority this way. Now, are your teams fully prepared in Paris and London?"

"Yes, but the evidence planting in London requires a bit more, or should I say deeper, background for credibility. We can pull the trigger now but if you can give me a couple more weeks…"

"Give me an update on Ashfin and Naryshkin first. Then I'll decide."

"As planned, Ashfin has built a very strong network in the IRG that will support his move up, while the economic disaster caused by both your sanctions and Pan virus has discredited the civilian government. With an economic and public olive-branch offered specifically to Ashfin from the AMU, the Iranians will be ready for a change to a leader with military experience," Ismail responded.

As dark and hardened as his own heart was, he was truly terrified to disappoint the AMU President. In private meetings, he had witnessed men literally fall dead in front of him as if an invisible knife had cut their throats. It never occurred to him that his own brother had died at the hands of this monster in a similar fashion many years ago.

"Naryshkin and his boss," he continued cautiously, "are slow to move. Their own economic crisis has put them in a non-aggressive posture, but for some of the same reasons as in Iran they can use a war to steer public attention away from it. In any case, they really need a prompt - something to pull them into the fray."

"I'm ready for that," the Leader grinned, looking down. "Tell Ashfin an olive branch is coming and tell Naryshkin to remember our deal. Then tell Yehuda to prepare for the Hook." Slowly, he turned his gaze on Ismail, knowing the fear that was burning in him. He smiled so gently that it caught the Minister of Information and Chief of Staff off guard.

"And I'll give you more time on the other two Heads of State. After all, they are only a means to an end."

Tel Aviv

Yehuda took the call from Ismail while going through Tamar's apartment. At Baruch's request, they planted evidence on her computer linking her to a false narrative that tied to his own secret communications with Ashfin. When found, she would look like a double agent, with handlers in Russia.

"It's a bad time. I've got to get this job done before my counterparts with internal security show up," he snarled.

"I'll make it quick. The President wants you to be prepared to execute the Hook and let Ashfin know that an economic boom will be headed his way when he needs it. Also, tell Naryshkin to remember the deal or there will be hell to pay," Ismail snarled back.

"OK, OK. I'm on it. After that, I'll be hunting down the two rats to whatever hole they've found."

"Good. It's on you and Baruch."

"It's Baruch's screw-up! I'm just the cleaner."

"Makes no difference. Just get it done."

A couple of hours later, Yehuda and a small team of agents were headed to Lina's home in Beersheba. In examining her computer files, they noted that some had been copied relating to an experimental shield of some sort.

Meanwhile, in the Israeli PM's office another call was taking place.

"You know, Mr. President, we have an unqualified support for your position," the PM offered. "Assigning your own staff member to be interim Chancellor of Germany is indeed sensible and will help stabilize the markets. However, I must say, we have some hesitation on turning over all our newest technology. We agreed to a gradual disarmament of our nuclear weapons, and we indeed are complying. However, we have made huge advancements in many scientific and technical fields that are still secret. To make them public is a risk to us and the Union. This was not part of our agreement."

"I understand, Ari. Nevertheless, I'm not negotiating with you. The Union needs your full cooperation to counter the military and economic threats posed by the Asian/Brazilian Bloc. You know, Israel cannot afford to be isolated like Turkey. Don't force my hand. Rest assured, I am totally your friend and as long as I'm in charge, the Union will defend you unconditionally. However, if you are not in the Union..." His pause was unnecessary for the PM. The point was made.

"I understand. It will be a tough sell here, nonetheless. I'll get back to you with an answer."

"Tick tock, Ari, tick tock," and the line went dead.

Ari was stunned. He couldn't risk the public outcry if he revealed this newest demand to his people. Jews and Arabs alike were virtually in love with the new President of the AMU. Yet he knew the truth, that his hand was being forced. No one besides a precious few at the highest security level knew what was at stake if he gave in. At first, he had welcomed the man's public support for Israel, yet recent moves were alarming and now this 'request' to share all their top-secret research and advanced tech was truly unprecedented.

In some respects, it would be even more dangerous than war. Robotics and AI in particular were so advanced in the labs that... He really needed help and advice, but the President's tentacles spread everywhere. Mossad had already told him that the hit on Chancellor Steiner was not from Turkey.

At the same time, he had reports that although most of the citizens were sensing their first breath of peace so to speak, more and more were so uncomfortable with the disarmament that they were leaving the country. Some seemed to simply disappear and were unreachable by friends or family. Ari considered it simply a by-product of change. The numbers weren't huge... yet.

A few weeks later, as a sign of good faith, and absent any other definitive answer, PM Ari Rosen authorized the release of technical research on a financial interface product. The software was complete and could be integrated everywhere with amazing simplicity from central banks all the way down to retail stores. The elegance of it was the way its distribution was so automated, being pushed through the internet in encrypted form and unwrapped at its destination all without human intervention.

The corresponding 'thin-client' app was worn on a person's skin. The only catch was that it had to be in a place that was easily accessible and would not stretch – it was, in essence, a software encoded tattoo.

The President was delighted but insisted on proof of the product's readiness via a nationwide test in Israel. Every financial and commercial entity was to implement it and 100,000 volunteers had to receive the mark on their hands for the trial run. The AMU would monitor the results. If proven reliable and effective, it would be used ubiquitously throughout the Union.

Meanwhile, the Council's technical agents secretly modified the code to render complete financial and administrative control to the AMU where ever it was implemented.

As news spread in Israel of the test process, some were motivated to leave the country and as a consequence, Yaakov and Tamar had even more residents at the refuge. Unfortunately, despite their efforts at secrecy, snippets of information on the wilderness site made its way back. The location remained a mystery but the existence of it caught the attention on Yehuda. As a consequence, he tasked his most trusted trackers with finding it.

Chapter 24

Wilderness

The facility buried deep within the mountain became home to many hundreds of people. Yaakov and Tamar emerged as the defacto leaders of the swelling group that now included doctors, engineers and even soldiers. Fortunately, their supply lines were active so that everyone's needs were met, however they were in danger each time they had to engage with their suppliers.

Abdul volunteered to go to Amman to replicate some of the supply relationships the team had established in Jerusalem and Beersheba. Yaakov agreed with the idea but first wanted Abdul to accompany him to get additional experience in vetting.

"Abdul, we will be meeting this time with some communications engineers. Are you sure you want to go?" Yaakov asked.

"Absolutely. You work so hard my friend. Anything I can do to help. I want to jump in."

"OK, we'll leave in two hours from the West entrance. But Abdul, I am also going to attempt to get a message to PM Rosen about Baruch. With what you've told us about the Council, it's clear that Israel is being betrayed by the very people charged with defending it. The Council agent that attempted to kill you, does he know you are still alive?"

"I'm not afraid, Yaakov. If I die, I now know where I'll be. But to answer your question, I can't be sure. If we get anywhere close to Rosen and if I'm with you, I'll be recognized so perhaps I should remain at a distance for that part of the trip," Abdul answered.

"Agreed. You will stay in the transport truck once we get to the government offices. This Mossad fellow you mentioned, what is his name?"

"We called him Yehuda, but he told me once it was not his real name."

"Is he close to Baruch?" Tamar queried.

"They work cooperatively, but they don't trust each other. Yehuda was the one who brought me to the Council. He used to protect me. Ironic, I think, since he's the kind of person who truly enjoys killing."

He looked down and shuffled one foot. Looking back up he added, "Yaakov, Rosen needs to know just how evil the AMU President is. He cannot be trusted. The Council has manipulated world events for a long time and now that he is in charge of the whole Union, I think there are some terrible things on the horizon for all of us. I was not privy to all their plans, but I'm convinced that Israel is in grave danger. I witnessed myself great, great evil in his eyes."

"You know, both Tamar and I felt that there was something wrong or suspicious with Baruch, but after learning from you about his treason, I want to ring his..."

"I think you mean trust the Lord, right?" interjected Tamar gently smiling.

"...neck," he finished. "Yep, you're right again. OK, Abdul, West entrance, meet me at two o'clock," he added and winked at his new fiancée.

Beersheba

The refuge was big enough for several thousand people, but in anticipation of coming world events, the new engineers were already at work designing expansions. Everyone sensed that although much of Israel was celebrating peace, catastrophe was imminent.

In order to better organize the new-comers' inbound process, and to carefully screen the people who wanted to come, the refuge needed enhanced communication and intelligence capabilities. Yaakov was amazed that it already had a powerful internet node operating off of a SpaceX satellite and an unhackable firewall. What he hoped to add was untraceable encrypted VOIP, Voice Over IP, to help communicate with potential refugees and with suppliers.

They also needed to arrange additional storage and receiving locations in about a dozen cities. Finally, he needed to get his hands on the parts necessary to further replicate the invisibility shield for all their transports. Currently, he only had one to spare.

First stop was in Beersheba. Yaakov's former co-pilot, Maj. Dahan, met them in a research lab at the University.

"Talia!" He shook her hand and then gave her a hug.

Happy to see him but surprised by the informality, she responded, "Yaakov. Where have you been? You took off for a couple days of leave almost six months ago. You said, this gear is critical, so I brought it. But what's going on??"

"Talia, are you positive you weren't followed?"

"Yes, but it's probably not coincidental that you ask because I have been followed frequently during the last month. Two men, not military. And my computer has been hacked. I told Cyber Security about it but got no answer."

"OK, look, I had to go into hiding because General Baruch sent his agents to hunt us down. We discovered his secret communications with someone in Iran..."

"Probably General Rouhani, Ashfin Rouhani,' interjected Abdul.

"Head of the IRG?! And who are you, sir?" Dahan asked.

"Talia, Abdul. Abdul, Talia." Yaakov said quickly; he did not want a lot of questions. Abdul shook her hand and smiled broadly. She looked closely at him with obvious recognition.

"That's crazy. And who is 'us'? You said, 'hunt us down,'" Talia queried.

"Do you remember Tamar from Cyber Defense on the Little Samson mission?"

"Wow! You did have it in you after all," she laughed. "She's hot."

"Very funny. She's my fiance now. And she's being hunted as well. Talia, Baruch is extremely dangerous, so you have to keep this under wraps. Understand? I can't emphasize that enough. Believe it or not, someday you may want to join us."

"Are you gone for good?"

"Don't know. But I have to get proof of Baruch's treason to the PM."

"So, what? You're going to walk in to the PM's office and say, 'Sorry, Sir, but your top General, an operational genius, is really a traitor' and then walk out??? You'll just screw up any chance of credibility," Talia asserted.

"She has a good point," added Abdul.

Yaakov thought for a moment. "Got a suggestion?" he asked.

"Respectfully, your information needs to look like it's coming from his own people, not an AWOL pilot."

"Good observation, Talia. Listen, you know how to contact me now. Stay under the radar on anything having to do with Baruch. Thanks again."

Abdul and Yaakov left with the comm gear in their truck.

Yaakov pondered what Talia had said and was convinced she was right. He had to convince someone the PM would trust to convey their intelligence. Then he got an idea.

"Abdul, I think we should get this thumb drive to Buki Carmelah, head of National Cyber Security. He was Tamar's boss or boss' boss, whatever. Anyway, Rosen will trust him."

He pulled the truck over and sent a secure text to Tamar. "How do I contact Carmelah? Does he know you?"

Almost immediately an answer came back. "He is in the PM's office. I've met him many times. Why?"

"We'll give the drive to him and tell him it's for the PM." He responded.

"Be really careful. He's very connected to Mossad but you're probably on the right track. The PM trusts him."

"Pray for us!" he answered.

"Always!!" she replied.

"OK, we're still going to head for the PM's office, but I'll find a way to get an audience with Carmelah," he said to Abdul who also seemed to be praying and nodded his head.

Within a couple of hours, they were parked at the Government Center just a kilometer or so west of the Old City in Jerusalem.

"I was thinking, Yaakov, I know Ari Rosen quite well. He might believe me if I gave him the drive," Abdul offered.

"And your supposed death would be over, dear friend. Then you would have a huge target on your back again. I know you're not afraid of that now, but remember, I'm going to help you find Aliya and your kids and that will be a LOT easier with you still around." He smiled at his companion.

Abdul grabbed his friend's shoulder. "Please be very careful."

"I will. I'll stay in touch with you along the way and hopefully we can get back soon."

Yaakov had been secretly honored by the PM after the Little Samson mission, so he knew his way. Surprisingly, his credentials were still active and although he got some extra scrutiny at one checkpoint, he was allowed to pass to the executive offices. There, to his delight, he saw Director Carmelah on his way to a meeting along with a couple of aides. He walked quickly to intercept them.

"Excuse me, Sir," he said as he stepped in front. One aide started to intervene.

"Hold on, Beni. I recognize this man," Carmelah said. "Katz, right? Little Samson. You've been missing for months. Do you know where our Tamar is?"

"Sir, short answer, yes. But I know I'm way out of line to approach you like this, but..." he showed Carmelah the drive, "I have information we, Tamar and I, obtained that proves General Baruch has been in secret communication with someone in Iran, probably General Ashfin Rouhani, in spite of the Pan outages there. We believe Prime Minister Rosen needs to know about it and that since he trusts you, I should give it to you first. Tamar and I both have been on the run from the General's agents because he knows we have this information. Please, sir. Look at it, listen to it. And please inform our PM. He must know."

Carmelah just stared at him. No answer. Then, he took the drive and said, "Follow me."

His aides, big men, took positions on each side of Yaakov and escorted him to an office without windows where he sat, hoping this was going to work. Carmelah was gone.

In a few minutes, two other men appeared and ushered him to a room several floors below ground. He guessed this was an interrogation room, probably Mossad. He waited till he was alone and then texted Abdul. "I've been detained. Probably Mossad. Get back to refuge."

Abdul bolted from the truck.

Office of the Prime Minister of Israel

Abdul was escorted by armed guards to PM Rosen's outer office. Along the way, many people recognized him and were aghast. No one was more surprised than Ari Rosen who met him there.

"You're alive!?"

"Ari, I am well. Although I have something important to tell you. Can we speak privately?" Abdul answered.

Rosen cleared the room and then brought him back into his private office.

"I can't believe it! Here you stand. My friend, your treaty has finally brought the peace we all longed for, though it has also brought some concerns," Ari said.

"Mr. Prime Minister, you have perhaps some concerns that you are not aware of as yet. That's why I am here. There is time now for me to relay to you only a few things. As soon as word of my appearance gets to the wrong people, I am not safe even in this office."

Rosen's face frowned and he leaned into the conversation.

"First, you must not trust the AMU Ministers and especially the President. If I have the time, I'll tell you more. Next, you have a senior IDF General who is a traitor to Israel, Baruch."

At this, Ari's face showed alarm.

"How do you know this?? Do you have proof?" he asked.

Abdul handed him the drive. "It is here. I know competent and loyal people who have proven here that he is in continual communication with someone in Iran and that person I am sure is General Ashfin Rouhani. I urge you to take appropriate action because I know the treason goes far beyond that."

Outside, gun shots rang out and then yelling to protect the Prime Minister.

In the seconds following, there was automatic fire and the office door burst open. A Mossad style assault team rushed into the room but both Prime Ministers were gone.

A few moments later, the rogue agents were trapped and gunned down themselves and a full lock-down on the government headquarters took place.

Government HQ sub-basement

Yaakov heard the alarms and saw his guards scramble to the upper levels. Taking advantage of the opportunity, he quickly exited and collided with a tall dark Mossad agent who seemed to recognize him. Immediately, the agent pulled out a knife and came after Yaakov who fled, looking for anything he could use as a weapon. Angrily, he recalled that his gun was confiscated at the entrance screening. The agent lunged and stabbed, missing him twice. With the second errant jab, Yaakov wrestled him to the floor receiving slash wounds in the process. Desperately, he held the agent's knife hand while they rolled.

Suddenly, something cracked upon the agent's head and he fell over on Yaakov and then to the tile floor unconscious. Over him stood Abdul, smiling. He tossed aside the remnant of the broken vase in his hand and helped Yaakov to his feet.

They ran down the hall for the elevator to the ground floor and as they ascended, the foggy agent shook his head and stumbled after them.

"Ari told me that if you were being held for interrogation, it would be down there. Are you all right?" Abdul asked, looking at the blood on his jacket.

"I'm fine. But what about the drive? We have to go back and get it," he answered.

"Don't worry about that my friend. Tamar made a backup copy for me just in case. I gave it to Rosen before we had to flee. I was indeed recognized, I think, and the Council's assets were sent to eliminate both you and me."

"Wait a minute. She did what?"

"She is a wise woman, my friend. Good foresight. If you were tortured and knew about it, well…"

"Of course. It was good that I didn't know. But what did Rosen say?!"

"He was stunned. And, obviously his security was compromised. I had no idea the Council had infiltrated so widely even in Israel."

"Did you tell him about the Council?" Yaakov asked.

"No. It would have been too much for him to take in. Anyway, I did not have the time."

"And now that you're 'alive again', you're going to be hunted."

"I know. But we did some real damage today and the Lord protected us. Right?" Abdul said happily.

They were careful to retreat to the truck or so they thought, but as they left the city, Yaakov noticed a black sedan following them. The tail continued at a distance as they proceeded south. At one point, hours later, approaching Eliat, he wondered if he had lost them or if he'd been mistaken. He pulled over and stopped the truck.

Reaching in the storage compartment, he grabbed the one spare SID, Stealth Invisibility Device, and powered it with the truck's USB interface. In a few seconds, the truck became invisible.

Less than a minute afterward, the black sedan passed them and as it did Yaakov saw four men inside. The driver was the agent who had tried to kill him. Fortunately, they seemed to have no idea they had passed by their 'prey' and continued on to Eliat.

"We will wait for evening to continue," Yaakov said to Abdul.

However, about twenty minutes later, the same car returned, driving very slowly while men in the rear and in the passenger-seat peered out their windows obviously looking for what they missed. Abdul's heart beat wildly, and Yaakov put his finger to his lips signaling silence. He couldn't turn off the engine or the SID would power off and they would be visible. He prayed that their engine noise would not give them away.

Then the car stopped, and one man got out. He went to the rear of Yaakov's car about fifty feet back and stared at the ground. They had pulled over on dirt and suddenly it struck both of them that the guy was looking at their tire tread marks leading right to them. He waved his hand at the driver of the other car to come look and as soon as the driver got out and headed their way, Abdul said, "It's Yehuda! He's an assassin!" Yaakov floored it, leaving a dust cloud behind then racing down the road toward Eliat.

Eliat/Aqaba crossing

Having passed the Israeli checkpoint, they went on to the Jordanian. Showing their Jordan Passes, they got their stamps and proceeded. Looking in his rear-view mirror, Abdul grabbed Yaakov's arm.

"Look behind. Do you see those men at the Israeli side running this way?"

Yaakov looked and reacted immediately. His truck sped away, eventually turning north. A few minutes later, Abdul asked, "Do you think we can lose them again. We don't want to lead them back to the refuge."

"You're right. I know it's not what you signed up for, Abdul, but we are going to have to make a stand and do it soon before they can even guess where we're headed. Hundreds of lives are at stake."

"Whatever you think we need to do, my friend."

They pulled on to 47 north and then highway 35 headed to Amman. At the 35/15 junction, they saw the sedan again on their tail. Yaakov plugged in the SID and they continued. Alarmingly, in a few minutes the device began to fail, and he could tell that they were visible again. The sedan approached at high speed and narrowed the gap to just a couple hundred meters.

Yaakov was not sure what to do. He had planned to set a trap for them closer to the city but at present they had no cover and no weapons. It was four against two and he was sore from his wounds. Abdul sat next to him and simply started to pray. The car full of attackers closed in. Gun shots rang out and the rear window shattered.

At this, Abdul started praying loudly, so much so that it shocked Yaakov. It was a mixture of Arabic and English. Yaakov was determined to lose them or die trying. He looked at Abdul who nodded his support and with that he made the truck virtually fly. He knew that at this speed, the engine could easily seize.

Suddenly, without warning, something like a meteor, a ball of fire, sliced through the sky heading straight for them. Both of them were terrified but looking back they saw the sedan behind braking hard. Thinking they were toast, Yaakov again pushed the truck to the limit putting 100, then 200, then 300 meters between them. Then BOOM, the meteor flashed by them and struck the sedan. The explosion knocked the truck sideways and it was a miracle they were able to stay on the road.

Yaakov stopped, then both he and Abdul got out to look back. Gawking at each other, shivers ran up and down and up again. Their mouths were agape as they turned their eyes to fasten in amazement on the fireball behind. The sedan was gone, vanished, and the road showed only a desolate crater where it had been.

"Do you think...?"

"Yes, it had to be."

As careful as they were, there was initially a threat of infiltration and treachery. A young man that Tamar had worked with infrequently in Cyber got a message to her via Ruben, one of their supply contacts who had been questioned and released by the police. Normally, he was careful, but on this occasion, as some of the first refugees were coming, he did not require them to surrender all electronics. Yaakov also learned the hard way to double-check this for he had trusted Ruben, who was still rattled by the police interrogation.

Their faux pas was exposed when, along the way south, Yaakov and his seven passengers pulled over for a pit stop. A few minutes afterward, six of the seven rushed back to the van and told him, in a panic, that a large black snake had come out of the desert and attacked Tamar's acquaintance, biting him in the leg.

Yaakov ran to see if he could help and found the man dead. He used his own burner phone to call an ambulance and then checked the man's pockets for ID. To his surprise, he found a cell which he quickly discovered to have a recently sent text message reading: "I'm in and heading to hideout. Will follow up as I know more. Loose security."

Yaakov was mad at himself. He destroyed the phone and tossed it in the desert. When he returned to the van, he asked everyone to empty their pockets and saw they were all 'clean'. After that, they never made any assumptions regarding old friendships or former associates. Clearly, the Council was trying to find them.

Currently, what they didn't know was that with Yehuda dead, the Council's leadership assets were stretched and thoroughly engaged in 'higher priority' international manipulations.

Ismail and the rest of the world thought Abdul was dead and Baruch had bigger issues to deal with than Yaakov and Tamar. And of course, no one knew of the scope of the refuge.

Chapter 25

Jerusalem

Ari Rosen examined what was on the drive repeatedly. Israel had never dealt with betrayal at this level or this extensive before. He argued with the head of the IDF for a long while over how to proceed. Disarmament had proceeded to the point that without experienced operational commanders, Israel's defenses would be in disarray. Baruch was not liked by his peers, but he was respected. After much unexpected debate, General Eizen stopped defending him. The burly IDF Chief of Staff acquiesced to Rosen's desire for the rogue military leader to be put under house arrest and his clearances to be stripped.

What Rosen did not anticipate was the degree of backlash against him from both the IDF command structure and Mossad. Unknown to him, the Council had far more assets in leadership positions than was even revealed on the drive.

At the same time, intelligence reports were pouring in. Iran's military leader, General Rouhani, Commander of the Guardians, was announcing a popular coup in which the civilian government would be "retired". In addition, the paramilitary Basij were being called up and armed for battle. Joining them together with the regular army, Iran was obviously preparing their entire military force numbering more than half a million for war.

In addition, he had data that showed suspicious or alarming troop movement in Sudan, Libya, Turkey, Syria, and worst of all, Russia. Except for Iran, all the troop movements were being done gradually and with no obvious connections, but Ari had a sense for this, and his gut was churning. He called for the Director of Mossad.

"Your reports are, in aggregate, extremely alarming or in error. Which is it, Yossi?" he demanded of the Mossad Director.

"May I answer?" Yosef Cohen, head of Mossad Collections, interjected.

The Prime Minister waited silently as did the Director.

"We don't know of any correlation yet but there is a common timing. All these actions began or accelerated as if in synchrony six months after the ratification of the Unity Treaty. The Sudanese/Ethiopian/Libyan activities are seemingly being coordinated by an Egyptian General, Berenike. Because of this, our surrounding flanks are facing forces numbering as many as 8.4 million including Russia."

Ari's eyes got big.

"That's about 14 to 1!" he exclaimed.

At this point, Yossi Shiloah, Director of Mossad spoke, "Cohen is using estimates based upon known active military personnel. As you know, my Caesarea department and Kidon unit heads were both killed in a freakish car incident in Jordan, so we are pushing our 'B Team' to fill in."

Cohen was put off by the implication but kept his cool.

"Back to my original question, Yossi. Good or erroneous data? And conclusions??" Rosen asked, now getting angry.

"You and I both know Eizen is losing control. Baruch's arrest has revealed many tentacles, many overt and subvert rebellions throughout IDF and my staff are trying to assist but, I have indications that Mossad may have been compromised as well and I do not know the extent. Even if we still had the Samson option, we'd be facing a world of hurt if the Russians become aggressive," Shiloah answered respectfully.

Tehran

"Naryshkin and his boss are dragging their feet. Dreamworks depends on them. I've done my part, now do yours." Ashfin sent the secure text to Ismail.

"I hear you, but he cannot be bullied. He is a powerful man with lineage all the way back to Peter the Great. His family has serious influence in Russia. The hook is ready, but we need the right circumstance to use it. Be patient." Was the reply. "By the way, Yehuda has not checked in, either off grid or dead. I'm using his back up to execute." He added.

Ashfin contacted Amir Gheedan, Lt. General and commander of the Iraqi Ground Forces Command the same way, "Gheedan, did you get your supply line freed up from the Americans?"

"Finally, yes. They have pulled all the way out." Came the reply. "But again, the Kurds are in the way. What's the plan there?"

"Trust me. They will only be a bump in the road when the time comes. They are survivors first and foremost."

Ashfin had assumed the position of Provisional Leader of the Islamic Republic of Iran as well as Commander in Chief of the Armed Forces. The country remained hampered by lack of control over technical systems, but he had prepared the nation for a conflict with the Little Satan, Israel, with massive manual logistics efforts. Iran had not signed the Unity Treaty and blamed the economic disaster they were in on Israel's attacks.

'Gheedan is an idiot. It's a good thing I'm in charge. And with Baruch out of the way, the Leader will look to me,' he mused.

The government of France had fallen. Protests organized and funded by the Council forced the country's leadership to flee and the new interim ministers agreed to effectively merge with Germany to avoid economic and governmental chaos. The AMU Leader was credited with this 'genius'.

"Two down and one to go," Ismail grinned before the Leader.

"Ismail, tell Ashfin to reach out now to the new Chancellor of the Franco-German coalition. I want them to be in the Dreamworks coalition. The Chancellor takes his orders from me. When Naryshkin is in place, he will think AMTO is taking the initiative."

"Genius, Sir. While Israel is praising you for making it possible to rebuild their disgusting temple, you are actually..."

"Don't try to guess my end game, Ismail," the Leader stopped him. "Just get it done."

"Of course, yes Sir."

"And why is Mahgoub still breathing?!" The Leader's eyes riveted on his Minister and Ismail felt his heart begin to fail.

"I... I'll handle it myself. I swear he won't be a problem. I'll f-find him, Sir," he eked out his reply while clutching his chest.

The Leader smiled darkly, "I'm going easy on you, Ismail, my friend. You realise that don't you?"

"Yes, Sir."

For a moment, the President looked down at the ground and said, "You know the source of my power, right?"

"Yes, yes, Sir - Allah."

"Wrong. So wrong." He laughed hideously. "Get out of here and get it DONE!"

Moscow

FSB headquarters was electrified with rumors. Some said a major war was imminent, some that the Franco/German Coalition was moving troops south, some even that Director Naryshkin had a recent meeting with Iranian, Turkish, Syrian and Iraqi leaders.

What no one knew yet was that the Russian President lay dead in his home. The very popular longtime leader of the nation died of an apparent heart attack, but the circumstances were suspicious as he had been in excellent health. In a matter of minutes, Naryshkin and the Minister of Defense were on the scene and shortly thereafter, Sergey Naryshkin was sworn in as the new President of Russia.

His predecessor's home became a crime scene after the coroner determined that an exotic drug 'cocktail' of calcium gluconate and potassium phosphate were injected in him. The blood workup was not the smoking gun. Rather the assassin spilled some of each chemical on the President's clothing, perhaps in a struggle or in a rush to inject the fatal doses each done separately.

Crime scene investigators found damning evidence that at least one of the attackers was from Mossad. DNA evidence matched that of a known assassin aka Yehuda Cohen. No one questioned that sloppiness on the trained assassin's part and when angry accusations reached Jerusalem, no one believed he was recently killed. The ensuing explosion of violent demonstrations in Moscow was heard around the world. With that and the threat of dirty bombs in Syria made with Russian-tagged nuclear waste, Naryshkin's hand was forced. No successful leader of the nation had ever been perceived as weak. Declaring emergency powers, he had the sixteen members of the former President's security detail executed and convened a meeting of his top military generals.

Additionally, he couldn't help but consider that in his covert meeting the same morning, the Dreamworks coalition leaders had agreed that if Russia led the way in an all-out military assault, he would own all the acquired Israeli wealth of technology and that their countries would switch their allegiance from the AMU to him. A new Russian empire would emerge to truly challenge the AMU.

So, when he also learned of Germany sending troops to Turkey, he was convinced that the AMU President was trying to steal away the opportunity.

The hook was set. The Russian 'bear' prepared to amble south.

Roma

"What are your assets telling you about Naryshkin?" the Leader studied Ismail as he asked.

"He is moving as planned."

"Good. Now, pull the trigger on the UK and tell Khan to be ready."

"And Israel?"

The Leader began to chuckle and then to laugh and then to laugh insanely.

Jerusalem

"Again, the answer is no, Ari. I cannot respond to your request," the AMU President said.

"Mr. President, respectfully, you are obligated by our membership. You must defend us against these overwhelming forces amassing on our northern and southern borders." Rosen had been pleading for nearly thirty minutes.

"Ari, you did not keep your end of the bargain."

"What do you mean?? We have disarmed all nuclear devices per the Treaty," Ari replied.

"My friend, my friend, you did not keep my bargain. You have not turned over your secret technology."

"We need more time, Mr. President. It is decades of research and development."

"You should have gotten in front of this, Ari. Now it is too late. I'm sorry. The AMU will not protect you under these circumstances."

"Is there no room for negotiation???" Rosen asked.

The line went dead.

Israel had all its traditional defensive forces on red alert but barring a miracle, they were no match for the impending assault. Never had the country been so outnumbered and unaided. Their only hope was a determined and experienced IDF.

No sooner had that thought flickered in his mind, but Generals Eizen and Baruch entered his office unannounced. There were no words exchanged.

A single shot rang out and Ari Rosen fell dead. General Baruch replaced his gun in its holster.

Epilogue

Once the AMU economic and political bloc was ratified by the 50 founding members it grew almost overnight to include all 139 countries in Europe, the Middle East, Africa and all the Western Hemisphere. Trade was fluid and nearly untariffed. No longer was any country concerned about trade imbalance as the AMU unified government controlled and balanced it for the whole Union.

Prosperity was unprecedented throughout Africa and Central America while the EU, North and South Americas remained healthy. Israel grew to have the second strongest economy behind the US due entirely to advanced technology and biosciences. There was of course just one currency and it was digital. There was still a clandestine group of elite and one Leader of it all.

Lalibela, Ethiopia

She gazed up into the night sky with its moonlight dancing upon the hills. In a few moments, she began writing:

"My dearest husband, so long it has been since we were together, but my heart still aches to be held by you. We, yes, all of us, have been in this beautiful and mystical place so high above the sea for many months now. We are being cared for by a very kind family of the Church. My dear one, travelers from Israel just told me of your death in Jerusalem, but last night I had a dream in which I saw you alive. You were radiant with holy light and you reached out your arms to us. I know you are alive and that we will one day be together again."

Aliya put the note in a brown envelope and entrusted it to Michael, a young traveler visiting from Beersheba.

"I will do my best to find him, Aliya," he vowed.

"And we will pray for you too," his mother added. "You have become so dear to us as is our precious Abdul."

Aliya hugged Vanessa tightly and cried gently in her arms.

Tasha smiled and her eyes sparkled with love.

Made in the USA
Lexington, KY
25 October 2019